MASTER B-1212

GARDEN OF THE GODS

A. A. DARK

Mad Girl
PUBLISHING

Master B-1212
Garden of the Gods
International Bestselling Author
A.A. Dark
Copyright © 2022 by A.A.Dark

All Rights Reserved

AUTHOR'S NOTE

Garden of the Gods is a collection of standalone novellas shadowing the lives of the Mistresses and Masters who occupy it. Although each main character will only have ONE book, they may appear in others throughout the series. Some stories will also have BDSM elements, but these stories are NOT BDSM. Mistress and Master is a title, showing nothing more than ownership. The scale of darkness in the stories will range from Pitch Black, Static White, to the extreme, Oblivion. Please be aware of this before you dive in. The rating will be in the blurb of each book. Trigger warnings are all over the board. If you are not comfortable with dark reads, please DO NOT read this series.

RULES

Rules are subject to change. If you neglect to follow these rules, you will undergo an investigation/trial where punishment is evaluated by the Board and Main Master, Elec Wexler. Punishment can range from fines to lockup in Hell Row to Death.

1) Keep your hands to yourself.

2) The only property you may destroy is your own. (slaves included.)

3) You are a number. Your peers are a number. Use them.

4) Respect your neighbor's privacy.

5) GOTG is NOT to be discussed outside of this facility.

GLOSSARY

W

Virgin slave. Wears a white robe during the auction.

B

Nonvirgin slave. Wears a blue robe during the auction.

D

Docile, drugged slave. Can be W or B. Heavily trained. Good for elderly or those with disabilities.

M

Male slave.

Crow

(fc: female crow, mc: male crow) Ruined, disfigure slaves. Breeders. Convicts fall into this category. Black robe during the auction. Usually the cheapest slave.

Blank slate

Mostly male slaves who have undergone forced indoctrination through various scientific methods. (Brainwashing, programming, training, etc.) Most remember their identity but have key parts of their past erased if it could pose a threat or alter their role as a slave. They're programmed to be focused solely on their Mistress or Master. They are made to be obedient, loyal, and protective.

*Master numbers written out throughout the stories are capitalized. (Ex. Twelve-twelve.) Also, the word Master throughout is capitalized. (Ex. Master Twelve-twelve.)

*Slave numbers written out will not be capitalized. The word slave throughout will not be capitalized outside from the beginning of a sentence.

"THE QUESTION THAT SOMETIMES DRIVES ME HAZY: AM I OR THE OTHERS CRAZY?" - ALBERT EINSTEIN

PROLOGUE
MASTER B-1212

Garden of the Gods
Colorado Springs underground facility

I was used to luxury. Galas. Elites. As I stared, watching my old friend walk the stage, I knew this was not like any high-class event I'd been to before...

"This is the beta run. Even though you have taken classes, and even though our slaves have been trained, no position as Master or Mistress is set in stone until you can prove you're worthy of the title. So far, you've passed enough tests to make it here to our first auction, but who are you? I'll tell you. You are the wealthy. The powerful. Influential. That got you here, but that's where it ends. Inside the Gardens, you have no name; you have a number. Your identity or status in the outside world means absolutely nothing. Zero. Here, there is no power or favoritism. This is my world, and you are no one. Let that sink in." He paused, staring us all down. "You are no one. The only thing that connects all of you is...*you're all fucking sick.*"

Laughter echoed in the large theater-type setting as I glanced around angrily. Crème-colored silk chairs decorated the

1

surroundings, and the pale lavender velvet accents invoked welcome. Just as my old friend, Main Master Elec Wexler did through his introduction as he continued. I could barely listen as my anger grew. I wasn't supposed to be here.

"Tonight is the first night of endless more auctions. A small majority of you come to us from Whitlock[1]. Take note, this is not that place. The rules are different. The location is different. Do not mistake me for your old Main Master. I am not Bram Whitlock. The Garden of the Gods will never fall."

Silence.

"For those who are new, let me explain how this works. We start the bidding with the white, or w's [2]for short. These are the virgins. From there, we move to the b's: or blue[3]." He paused, raising one of his eyebrows sarcastically. "*You guessed it*: not virgins. The d's[4] will follow. They're docile, trained, and good for those who are looking for a long-term slave. Lastly, come the black, or as we call them, the crows[5]. They're not your typical slave. These are the cheap, buy-one-get-one-half-off sort of deals. They are the convicts. The disfigured. The breeders. Some are plain repulsive." He shrugged. "And if you're into it, old. You get it. Like I said, not typical for a place where beauty and sterilization are usually the standard."

Sterilization? Well, that made things convenient.

"For the Mistresses or those looking for our programmable, 'blank slate' [6]males, your auction is just through that door off to the right. The information was in your packet, but just in case you missed it, these are the males who have had portions of their memories erased. They know who they are, but they only remember what we want them to. We'd like to think when it comes to security issues, we've learned from the past. Like I said before, we're in the beta stages, but we're assured these male slaves are safe. Since we're doing our own trial run, you can get them at a steal. They will take orders. They will obey no matter what the demand is. Use your imagination. If you're still having trouble understanding, read more about each of these in the pamphlet."

He turned, pointing, but continued as I glanced around taking in celebrities I knew but had never personally met. There was a lot, ranging from sports stars to musicians. Actors. CEOs. I had even spotted one of those religious TV ministers made rich from their zealot supporters.

"Some of you are here to spill blood. Some want sex beyond the norm. Here, there are no rules. What you buy is yours. Do with it what you will. Fuck it. Kill it. Eat it."

Elec walked down the length of the stage. I took in his black fitted suit and matching black button-up shirt and tie. His dark hair was shorter than it used to be, and his handsome features had only grown over time. He was comfortable as he addressed us, and I didn't miss the pride that seemed to radiate from him. He was taller than I remembered, but he was just as serious as he stared us down. If I didn't know any better, I could almost mistake him as his cousin, Bram Whitlock[7]. Their resemblance from a distance was uncanny.

"If you look down the arm of the chair, you will see a button. Do not." He stopped, turning in a slow circle to view everyone in the room. "Let me say it again, so I'm not accused of not making myself clear. *Do not*...press that button unless you are sure you want to bid. Also...do not continue bidding if you don't have the money. Here, there's no such thing as accidents. If you bid, you buy. If you can't pay, I will take my payment however I see fit. Your business. Your house. Your hand." His eyes narrowed. "*Your life*. I am not your friend. I am not going to take it easy on you. If you cross me, you're dead. If you lie to me, I will cut out your tongue, and then you will die. Honesty is everything. Remember that."

My lids lowered through his violent threats, but I wasn't overly surprised. Elec had always held a sinister aura, but maybe that's why we'd gravitated towards each other.

3

"The rules are easy, but acceptance into the Garden of the Gods comes at a price. You signed a contract to get this far. You know the dos and don'ts. Memorize them. It could mean your life if you forget."

Lights raced the length of the circumference, illuminating the edge of the floor, and running over the top arches of multiple doorways. Gasps and chatter filled the theater and heads spun from the stage to the nearest entrance as a line of the most beautiful women adorned in sheer, white robes awaited their cue.

"Now that we got that out of the way; prepare to empty your wallets. This is the fun part. You're about to have your wildest, bloodiest dreams come true. Happy bidding, Masters and Mistresses. I have no doubts you'll enjoy."

MASTER B-1212

Maybe I should have left. I would, if I could, but I knew the rules. A slave was mandatory, but I couldn't force myself to go that far. To commit to pushing the button was to admit I had a problem. I didn't. Not any I was willing to acknowledge. I was an asshole. I loved inflicting pain…That did not mean I was supposed to be at the Garden of the Gods with all these depraved monsters. Maybe I was the only one in this city of nightmares who didn't want to be here. Wasn't everyone all smiles and excitement? Not me. I'd spent the last few days trying to figure myself out. It crossed my mind that there was a chance I was so far gone, I was delusional to the truth. Didn't most people who had issues live in denial? Was that me?

Perhaps.

Sadly, I couldn't change the direction my life had taken on the outside world. It was littered in disaster with accusations. One woman. Three. With money they disappeared with their lies, but when my lifelong friend died, she nearly brought me down with her. My world fucking stopped, and my dad…well…he didn't give me a choice. He brought me to Elec. The entire situation was to get me out of the headlines and to safely sate my needs, but I never fucking expected this. I didn't want it, but the son of the Vice-President couldn't be going around roughing women up, even if they did ask for it. Or *fucking beg*.

"I told you, I'm not bidding. There's nothing wrong with me."

Elec rolled his eyes, content to hide with me up in my boxed seat for a few minutes away from the others. He loved his position here as Main Master, but I didn't blame him for wanting to stick his knife in most of these spoiled Masters and Mistresses. I hadn't been in the main building for more than half an hour before I already had a confrontation. There was clearly going to be some issues on appeasing these pampered fools who thought they could have their way on anything.

"I promised your father I'd take care of you here. If you don't bid, so help me, I'll gift you with three. One slave, Rob, that's all you need."

"I can't believe I'm even here. You do realize how fucked up this is, right?"

Elec threw me a look. "Coming from someone who nearly just killed a woman. If you were anyone else, you'd be in jail right now. You're lucky for her accident. Even your daddy couldn't have saved you from this one had she pressed charges."

"She never would have. I didn't do anything Porsha didn't want. Hell, she cried in pleasure for hours for me to kill her. That's how far gone she was. That accident was no damn accident at all. She loved her pills; she just loved my cock more. When I refused her request and left, she did what she felt she had to. She's been suicidal for years. I'm actually quite upset over the entire thing, Elec. I don't find any of it convenient at all. It was a tragedy through and through. I had needs; she had needs. We sated our fucked-up desires with each other until the end."

"Is that what you're telling yourself, Rob?" He shook his head, pity creeping into his expression. "Find a slave. I won't tell you again. You better leave here with someone tonight or come morning you won't have a choice. Embrace yourself. It's all you can do now."

I crossed my arms over my chest as I glared at the slaves who took their turn walking to the stage. He had no idea what the fuck he was talking about. I wasn't like the people here. I wasn't sick; I just preferred other things…darker things. That wasn't illegal, but perhaps not having to worry for once would be nice. Not that I was about to admit that to Elec.

"I hate you. I've hated you since back in college when you left me at the club to go home with those two blondes from that football team. Then, not a year later when you beat me out for that internship with Trux. You didn't even need it. I had appearances to keep up, you know."

"I did you a favor. You would have hated it all. You did just fine with Dawson LX. Hell, you're fucking nearly running that place."

"I still hate you. The blondes; you could have shared."

"You were under too much heat over the brunette you took home the week before. Jesus, Rob. Are you not seeing a pattern?"

"I wouldn't have hurt them. Josie just wanted the cash and hated my father. If anything, that one was politically motivated. I'm telling you, you got this all wrong. What happened with those blondes?"

Elec let out a breath. "I gave one to Trevor. He married the cuter, insatiable one. Timber? I can't remember if that was her name; it was too long ago, and I haven't seen him in a decade. Why are we even talking about this? Take a look at what's before you now. You won't find anything better. Not just in looks, but in behavior. We train the females slaves well. For any situation, really. They know they'll probably die, but if you didn't want to go that far, one could make you happy. They'd even be grateful."

"If I wanted to settle for one person, I'd marry Lesli Morrison like my dad wants."

7

"She is quite the looker. Excellent pedigree."

"I'm not interested in bloodlines. Besides, I'll never marry."

"Do. Don't. Whatever floats your boat. If you do find that it becomes appealing for your life here, the chapel is on the fourth floor. We offer everything, so long as it stays secret behind these walls, and keeps your ass out of trouble. We're a one stop shop for pretty much anything."

"I've noticed. Fucking stables, Elec? Seriously? Are you planning on hosting a hunt? A rodeo? This place is beyond fucked up."

"Actually, yes. Our human hunts are Mondays, Thursdays, and Sundays. If you thought bestiality was bad, you haven't explored this place thoroughly enough. I encourage you to look around. Broaden your mind. Accept there are things in this life we can't help. Why hide from them or continue living in the hell of denial? You're fucked up; I'm fucked up; We're all fucked up. It is what it is. Accept and embrace. It's the only way."

"You sound like a twisted postcard or commercial."

"I guess I do. I'm proud of this place. If you saw how far we've come in the last year and a half, you'd understand. It's quite amazing, really."

"You're enjoying this way too much." My head shook, but my stare stayed ahead. A new white veil appeared, just the same as the rest. Where most had skittered to the stage, she walked tall, despite her average height. There was nothing rushed about her. One step. Another. Her hips swayed as men reached out grabbing, but she didn't so much as give them notice. Red hair shone through the sheer white, and my eyes narrowed as I took in her nude, curvy form. Porsha had had red hair, but not like that. Where my lifelong friend's was more orange, this woman's was more of a deep mahogany. Not to mention, it was longer and wild with tight curls. Not close to Porsha, but close enough to interest me as I watched her reach the stage and drop the top down to reveal her face.

Ivory skin was flawless. Maybe I expected freckles like Porsha, but I didn't see any from where I sat. She had overly full lips and big, round eyes. Whatever their color was, I couldn't tell, but they didn't appear brown.

A slight buzz to my chair had my gaze snapping down. My light was on from bidding. I threw Elec a look, even angrier than when I'd been told I had to come here. There wasn't anything wrong with me. I didn't want a slave. I didn't want anyone.

"You seriously didn't just do that."

"You like her."

"You're wrong."

"I'm never wrong, Rob. I can't afford to be in the Gardens." He hit the button again. "You like her; you need someone. It works. Kill her if she doesn't make you happy. Kill her if she does. I don't care but have a slave as an outlet because you're not allowed back to the outside world until you face who or what you are."

"Did I say I hate you because I fucking despise you right now." I knocked his hand away, replacing it with mine.

"You're just mad because as much as you want to control your urges, you're having trouble. I saw the cuts and bruises you left on Porsha. I'm surprised you didn't break her neck. You lost it, Rob, and you can't afford to do that up there. You don't have to worry about it anymore." He stood. "I know you don't like being here but accept this life. You may come to find it helps you out in here," he said, tapping against his temple, "a lot more than you could imagine. Then you can go home and return when you need to. That's why we're here...*to help*."

"Go help Mr. Fredricks. I saw that weirdo earlier. I hate how we all associate in the same circles. He's a doctor for crying out loud. What's he even doing here? Working? Keeping tabs on me for my dad?"

Elec threw me a look, shaking his head. He couldn't go into detail if he wanted to. That's not how the role of the Main Master

9

worked. Secrets between him and the people who paid for their spot required a level of privacy I expected myself.

"Master Sixty-three. He bypassed the w^1's and went right for the d^2's off in the back. He just bought a cute little brunette with a bob cut. Pickup won't be any time soon for him, and it has nothing to do with the money. I believe he'll be one of our long-term Masters, but..." Elec's eyes narrowed. "We'll see how this first slave turns out for the dear ol' doctor. I'm a bit weary of him. I think he has more secrets than the ones he's disclosed." He paused. "Better get to clicking, Rob, or you're going to lose your slave."

"Stop worrying about me. Go work or something."

He laughed, winking. "Breakfast at The Six. It's on floor nineteen and by invite only. I'll put you down. Eight o'clock."

"Yeah, fine."

A growl left me as I smashed the button. I didn't even care how high the numbers were as Elec walked away. My stare went back, staying fixed on the woman's face as I kept increasing the stupid bid. She was young. Maybe twenty. Fuck, I hoped at least twenty because young was not what I was into. Even early twenties were pushing it, but it's not like I was choosing her to date. Like Elec said, she was an outlet. I needed one of those if I wanted to return to my regular life. A life I didn't even care to think about either. It was all a fucking joke. Maybe some time here wouldn't be so bad.

My Master number flashed on the screen as I once again clicked. Turning to look behind me, I made sure Elec was gone before I picked up the binoculars that were sitting on a small table next to me. The slave up close had me swallowing hard as I took her in.

From above, she was gorgeous. Her aura couldn't hide the sophistication she projected. It made no sense outside of her looks, but she felt...more. Worthy of so much more than this. I took in her features again, correct on my assessment as I moved to her eyes. They weren't brown but a vibrant emerald color. I wasn't sure I'd ever seen anyone with eyes so green.

Moving down, I took in the column of her neck, fixating for longer than I should. When I got to her breasts, I felt no shame for lingering. They were on the smaller side. Maybe one handful. Maybe slightly more. They weren't as big as I liked, but they'd work. Going further, I took in the curve of her hips. She'd had an ass too if I could remember correctly. She was thicker than most of the slaves, powerful-looking thighs. Powerful, yes. She'd be a good fighter. More of a challenge. The longer I looked, the more I liked about her. So much so, I hadn't even realized how aggressively I was hitting my button. Aggressive...like I liked.

W0023

"What is this? Is this for real?"

The two men who stood before me looked at each other, and then back to the paper. A proper slave would have kept her head down. A good slave would have done what she'd been taught. That would never be me. I was not raised to cower or be controlled; I had been meant to lead. Just because I had been taken out of that life didn't mean I'd start now.

"Let me see that." The taller man I knew as the Main Master took the file. There was confusion drawing in his lips, and even a small amount of disbelief crinkling his brow. As he scanned down the profile meant for my new Master, he appeared just as confused as the man who bought me. "How peculiar and rare. I should have known about this." He looked up, pinning me with hard eyes. "Taken from a caravan? You're a gypsy?"

My native tongue poured from my lips. Curse words my mother would have beat me for if she would have heard.

"Great. She doesn't speak English, either? Elec, you've got to be fucking kidding me."

"She speaks English," he bit out. "Our slaves are evaluated

and trained. If she didn't speak the language fluently, it would be in her chart. *It's not.* A gypsy though, really?"

At his question, I allowed my eyes to cut away from him in dismissal. It was a mistake. Fingers twisted in my hair painfully, forcing me to my knees as the Main Master's other hand came around to lock on my face.

"I asked you a question. You dismiss me once more and you can kiss this opportunity goodbye. I'll replace you, and you can burn. Answer. *In English.*"

Something close to a growl and cry left me as I welcomed the pain and jerked against him. He wanted answers, but I could barely think straight to put English words together.

"You insult me. Gypsy is a dirty word. I am Romani. Clara Orlah. I am a prize. Betrothed to *the* Donavon Bordelli. Opportunity? This is an opportunity? Burn me."

"Bordelli. I've heard of them. Gypsy royalty. I should have charged more for you. There's plenty of men who would love to break your spirit." He let go of my face, reaching into his pocket. With his teeth, he twisted a top free, rolling more oil over my forehead while I jerked against the hold again. Within seconds, emotion began to fade. Heat flared in a roll of pleasure, but I still fought.

"Her accent sounds Russian or something."

"Maybe a little, but it's not that," the Main Master said, letting me go. "The Bordelli have their own language. I've heard about this. Not much, they're very secretive, but they travel around in groups. Some are big; some are small. These people live a completely different lifestyle than most. They're very superstitious. That's what I hear."

"*They.*" I made a spitting motion off to the side before rolling my eyes. "You know nothing. The Bordelli are like no one. We are our own. We are right."

"Sure you are." The Main Master's mouth tightened into a line at his disapproval. He looked over, uncertainty masking him.

"I bid on her first. I'll allow you to cancel or replace her, but only this once. I'm not doing this as your friend. This was my mistake."

Brown eyes scanned my face. It wasn't angry or annoyed like the Main Master's. There was amusement. Even a slight smirk on his handsome features and it tried to vanish under the question but failed.

"No mistake. I can handle her. We're good."

Surprise flashed over his face, but the Main Master shrugged, almost seeming to understand something I didn't. "If you say so. The oil will keep her calm for a little while, but she'll be a lot more trouble when it fades. Are you sure?"

"Absolutely."

"Okay. Have fun with that. It might be exactly what you need. Let me know if you run into any issues. I'll get you your own vial if you need it."

The Main Master handed over my file, stepping back. "Don't forget about breakfast. There are shackles in the room on the floor. I made sure to have some put on your bed too. Keep her locked up while you meet me, or your day will be a hell of a search. She's a runner, and she'll do it at the first opportunity. Mark my words. I'll see you at breakfast."

"I'll be there." He turned to me as Elec walked away. For seconds his eyes studied me. When he shrugged out of his suit's jacket and wrapped it around my shoulders, I let caution come back to the forefront. He was handsome, yes, with his dark hair and dark tanned skin, but he was a lot older than me. Not old, in the sense. He couldn't have been but in his early thirties, but still, I couldn't see myself choosing him if I would have met him outside these walls. Maybe it was because I'd been so sheltered. Truthfully, I had been downright clueless before I got here, even concerning whether I wanted to marry Donavon, but I didn't have a choice for fear we'd be banished. After all, we'd been promised to each other since I was ten. I couldn't back out. It was the way things were. Our views on all things were so different than here. Just like a lot of daily habits people did so freely. Food. Eating. Rituals. Showering. Everything they did was so carefree where the Bordelli were strict on cleanliness. Here was so...wrong. It all scared me and promised of hardship to come. I didn't know what to believe. We didn't talk about things like sex or even periods. It was forbidden. Dirty in the Bordelli's eyes. I had been so unprepared for life. For *marriage* after what I'd seen in the shower room with one of the b's and a guard. I wasn't sure what to think about any of it.

"Stand up."

I obeyed as my new Master pulled at the lapels, tightening the jacket around me even more. I reached, holding to it as the damn thing swallowed my frame. Swaying, I quickly caught myself.

"I haven't decided if I want to call you slave. You said your name was Clara?"

"Yes."

Hesitation.

As he began to walk, I followed. Had I expected him to be nice? No...I'd been prepared for death up until the minute the man said hello. It was so strange. All of this was. Nothing was making sense with how foggy I felt.

"What do I call you?"

"Master is fine. I didn't think to check your file. How old are you, Clara?"

The need to argue over his title was there, but for some reason I held my tongue. I had my name, so what if he wanted to be called a Master. At least I was winning the smallest victory. "I just turned eighteen."

He winced. "And a virgin I'm guessing from the white robe?"

"Shh. You shouldn't say such things." I flicked my wrist, swiping through the air, more trying to wave the bad word away.

15

Not that it was bad, but more something you didn't say or even talk about unless you wanted to invite negativity or illness. It was that way with anything dirty, and I'd be no part of it if I could prevent myself. He smiled again, but it was quickly replaced by a more serious expression. One that had me swallowing back fear.

"Don't worry about that, then. You won't have to bother yourself over it much longer. You speak your mind a lot. Do you like to fight, Clara? Would you say you're very strong?"

"I..." Silence took over me as we joined others who were waiting on the elevator. I searched my mind, trying to find some way to answer my new Master. Screams immediately cut me off. Warmth splattered over my face causing me to gasp at the surprise. I wasn't even able to reach for the wetness before large arms were around me, pulling me out of the way. The shrieks were deafening. I wasn't sure if it was me yelling out or the girl who clutched to my arms, howling from the lacerations stretching across her face. Skin was split above her eye, and a part of her cheek was hanging in a massive chunk, swaying as she tried to get closer. The bone over the bridge of her nose was exposed, and I joined in her screams, not sure what was happening.

"You dare attack your Master?"

The roar that came from behind her vibrated every cell in my body as it got closer. My eyes rose, coming head on with evil. A man stomped forward, scratch marks down his face, dripping blood. He wielded a weapon closely resembling a spiked handheld rake. As he reached back to swing again, me and the girl were spun in the opposite direction. I fell to the floor with her still holding onto me just in time to see my Master slap the weapon away.

"Are you fucking mad, old man?"

"That's my slave."

"And that's mine you're about to tear into to try to get to her.

Keep that shit in your place or watch what the fuck you're doing." My Master turned his enraged expression to me. "Get on the elevator. *Now.*"

"I can't. I w-won't. She's hurt—" Fingers still clawed at me, ripping the jacket from my shoulders as I tried to break myself free, but not so I could leave her. Blood beaded my forearms from her nails as she continued to wrap around me in her panic. She wouldn't let go so I could try to put myself between her and the man who was no doubt about to kill her.

"Clara. *Slave.* Now."

More curses left me in my native tongue, and I couldn't think clearly enough to find the words in English to try to calm her. My new Master didn't give me the chance. He grabbed the girl by her bicep, tossing her to the side as he jerked me to stand. Before I could even look back at the girl being beaten again, he was already pulling me on the elevator. That did not erase the cries or thunks of impact from the spiked rake I could hear in the distance. Her screams increased, only fading as the elevator door shut.

"I can be nice all day long but when I tell you something out here, you listen. Do you understand me?"

"You condone murder? You think es' okay to beat and torture innocent girl?" My words twisted around themselves as I fought through the adrenaline and terror that was suddenly making itself known. My eyes were blurred by tears, and all I could see was the marred flesh on the girl's face. She had to be my age if not younger. And she was so afraid. Would that be me? Is that what I had ahead of me?

"*What I think* is that was none of our business. What I *think* is outside of our apartment, you keep your mouth shut and your opinions inside that head of yours before it stirs up even more trouble. Inside, I can deal with it. Out here, you don't cross me. You obey and listen." His head shook. "I swear to fucking God, everywhere I go there's always something."

He reached into his pocket, pulling out a card as the door reopened on the sixteenth floor. We didn't make it two doors before he slid it in and pushed the barrier. When I hesitated to go in, he flattened his palm on my back, practically pushing me inside.

Darkness.

The sound from his shoes moved further away as I stayed cemented to the floor. When the light filled the space, I still didn't move.

"You're bleeding. I should clean you up."

My lip quivered despite I could barely reach my emotions. I didn't need to for my body to know I'd been traumatized by what I saw. That girl wouldn't be getting cleaned up. Maybe she was dead by now. She'd be wishing she was if she survived the night. Hadn't this been what we'd been warned about now for months? Prepared for? My stomach turned as I grasped at what I could decipher through the oil.

"Clara." His voice softened as he headed back towards me. "You're okay. I know you're shaken up, but this is your life now. I'm afraid from here on out, things aren't going to get any better. Come...I think there's some antibiotic ointment in the bathroom. We'll put some on your arms after your shower."

I took a step back, hugging tighter to my chest. The action had my new Master's mouth twisting in disapproval.

"We've gotten off on the wrong foot. I find when shit gets complicated to be blunt. How's that? Are you good with me being upfront and honest?"

"Honest?"

"That's right. Let's be as crystal clear as possible. Does that work for you?"

Nodding, I wasn't sure I liked where this was going but wasn't honesty important? Wouldn't it prepare me for what was to come?

"Great." He gestured to the black leather sofa. I took a seat, watching as he sat on the opposite end as me. "Let's start out with who we are. You're Clara, and me, I'm your Master."

"I don't like it."

His features tightened but he gave a stiff nod. "I'm not giving you my real name to use. I don't care how private this place is. This isn't me anyway, this is a...predicament, not my chosen reality, and sadly I can't leave here until I face it. That's what I'm doing. I didn't choose this, but I have no choice. I'm your Master, whether you like it or not."

Heat flushed my skin through the conflicting pride. "Fine. Master."

"Good. Now we discuss us. Your job as a slave is to do whatever I want. You didn't ask for this. I'm aware of that, but my position here is a Master, and I have to play that role too if I'm going to be allowed to leave."

I blinked through what any of it meant.

"So...you want to kill me so you can leave?"

"What? No. I don't have to kill you to leave. I just have to be honest with myself and accept...things." He stopped, anger forcing him to his feet as he paced. "I didn't want you. I didn't want anyone, but I have problems that apparently need to be confronted. It's bullshit really, but I can't escape it. The Main Master won't let me leave until he thinks I have this under control, and I'm afraid that's not going to fare too well for you."

"But no death?"

"No death," he repeated.

My lids were growing heavier as I tried to force more questions I needed answered.

"Why are you here? What must you face?"

My Master slowed, coming to a stop a few feet away.

"Apparently, I hurt women and it's an issue. To me, they asked for it. They even liked it. There have been instances where they've come forward claiming otherwise. My dad thinks I'm delusional. I don't think I've done anything wrong."

"Hurt? How?"

His eyes lifted up as if there were so many he didn't know where to begin.

"Well, I'm very handsy. I like the throat."

It took me a good minute to understand what he meant. "You choke women?"

"I do. Not to the point of them passing out. Not entirely anyway." He swallowed hard. "I can't believe I got a virg—"

"Shh!"

"I should have got a blue," he snapped. "I shouldn't have gotten anyone. You're not ready for this. Not even close."

"What else will you do?"

"I can't say *virgin*, but I can tell you what I'm going to do to you?"

"It's all dirty," I ground out. "Bad, but I have to hear. What else?"

"The normal stuff. Some not so normal stuff. Fuck, I don't know. Spanking, pain stuff. Choking. Hair pulling." His eyes sliced over to me just like his words. "Cutting. Knife stuff. Burning. Nothing overly bad, just...pain stuff. Fighting. I like a good fight. I probably like that the best of all."

Being undressed suddenly wasn't sitting so well with me. This man, for as calm as he seemed now, was a completely different person when he wanted to change. That terrified me. How long would it be until I saw that man? Would I even be the same after he finished? Pain didn't bother me...the way it was inflicted did.

MASTER B-1212

Well, if she didn't want to run before, she sure as hell did now. Despite her drugged state, Clara looked like a deer in the headlights. Like one of the slaves here being cast into a field to be hunted. She was so eager to take off in a dead sprint. Sad thing was, I was waiting. *Ready*. A part of me even wished she did. Had I really turned out as bad as I'd been told by all those around me? Had I missed my own drop in sanity that I fell into the brink long ago? Did I, Robert Lawrence Delgado, belong to the Garden of the Gods? The question alone was enough to turn me off.

"I think we're done discussing things for the time being. Shower."

Hesitation.

"Slave. Clara." I gestured to the room trying to ignore how that word so easily escaped from my lips. "I will not be attacking you in the shower. You're safe for the time being. I need to make some calls anyway. I'll stay in here. I believe Elec mentioned clothes in the closet. Go find something while I take care of some business."

"You'll stay out here?"

"I didn't say that. I said I'd stay out of the bathroom while you showered. That room belongs to me. I'm the Master, remember?"

A collection of emotions flickered, but none I cared to pick apart. My focus wasn't on Clara or sex right now. Not really. There were unresolved issues I had on the outside world. Things I just couldn't walk away from. And hadn't that been what happened? Porsha overdosed and died, still wearing my marks two days later, and all hell broke loose. I was swept out of the city so damn fast and flown here, I hadn't even been able to call anyone besides my secretary. Lauren said she'd take care of my appointments for the next few weeks, but business didn't work like that. I'd be lucky to have a fucking job when I returned.

Footsteps padded off into the distance as I flipped the odd-looking phone over, trying to see what made it so different than my own. It was flat. Average size. Why hadn't I been able to bring in mine? Maybe they worried one of these morons would snap pictures or something. Not like they couldn't from this thing. It had a damn camera, but I had to leave it in the apartment when I left to the outside world so perhaps that was it. None of it made any damn sense to me, but with all the security measures it took to get inside, perhaps they had it all sorted out. As I hit my secretary's number, I quickly discovered the answer. No service. The phone didn't even ring. What the fuck was this shit?

My eyes closed as I took a deep breath. When I opened them and dialed my father's number, same thing. Nothing. I snatched the packet from the coffee table, pulling out the papers that had been thrust at me when I arrived.

Rules.

Menus.

Events.

Shops.

Numbers…I scanned over them, seeing Elec's but not even wasting my time to call him. This phone was obviously only able to work within this place. Every number I came across began with a pound symbol. That didn't help me to connect with the outside world. The realization only had my blood heating even more.

Water sounded in the distance, so quiet I could barely hear it. I didn't have the patience to worry about the slave right now. She was cute. Tempting even, but for what? Did I even know what I wanted? It's not like I combed the streets, hunting out my next victim to choke and beat. Women came to me. They were never in short supply, but even that didn't mean I behaved in a way that would warrant me here. Hell, Porsha was the only one I'd even been with in the last few months, and that was mainly because I knew she was falling deeper into depression. She'd been my best friend. My true best friend, and I loved her. Maybe not the traditional way, but I would have done anything she asked me. Anything...but kill her like she'd wanted. Hadn't she been begging me at the end?

Red hair flashed before me, spanning over the light pink sheet she'd had on her bed. My hand was around her throat, holding, not squeezing.

"Do it, Rob." Tears were pouring from her swollen eyes as I fucked her slow. Fucked her back to life? I could have only wished she was still the lively woman who'd been the light in every room she walked in. That light had burnt out years ago. Burnt out possibly because of me. Maybe she thought we'd become more. Maybe she thought she could get over her assault back in college. She never even told me the story behind that, but I knew it was bad. She hadn't been the same for quite some time, and a huge part of me blamed myself. I should have pushed more for the truth. I should have tried to get it out of her. I knew Porsha. She would have never told me if she didn't want to, and she never did.

"Rob. I'm waiting. Rob." She loved my hand around her throat, but she didn't want me to stop this time as I held it around

her securely. Holding, not choking. What she begged for I couldn't do. Almost, but I stopped in time when I almost hadn't. *"Please. Rob. I can't do this anymore."*

"I can't do this anymore." I squeezed my eyes shut, repeating the last thing she'd said to me. I finished fucking her, but she didn't so much as tell me goodbye as I'd left. Just her pleas and finality. They kept repeating the entire time, and hadn't that been why I'd gotten so angry towards the end? I had been drinking that night, but it was clear what happened. I hadn't been so far gone that I'd been oblivious to the truth.

Minutes went by as I mindlessly paced. Even when Clara headed back into the living room wearing a long nightshirt, I didn't stop or give her much attention. There had to be a way to figure this all out. If I could only think, I could come up with a plan.

Sounds were soft in the kitchen, pulling me from my focus. The slave was looking around, albeit very cautiously as she watched me. For some reason that only made me angrier. I was so sick of everyone looking at me like I was some sort of snake. As if I were ready to attack and no one was safe. I wasn't a good man. So what. You could fuck the devil without losing your soul. You could have rough sex without killing. It's not like I was some murdering monster. Unless I was, and I was too crazy to see it.

"I'm hungry. I was too nervous to eat. May I…Master?"

I waved my hand as if I didn't care, too concerned over my own grief and needs to worry about hers. I just wanted her gone for the meantime; away from me so I could sort this out. I'd only just lost Porsha. Why the hell had I even been tempted to purchase her? Because of her hair? Because she reminded me of a woman I loved as much as I hated?

Or maybe I should face the truth. Maybe Elec was right, and I knew I was out of control. I was sated right now and fresh off from committing my deeds. The time was going to come when the inferno in me burned once again, and now that I had a free hall pass to do as I wanted, I wasn't so sure how long I'd be able to hold it off again. I could, but would I really want to if the opportunity presented itself?

I took in the damn curls that were already lifting. Tight little spirals wound round and round, twisting and turning through their long length as they were already beginning to show signs of their wildness. Her hair was unruly when it was dry. Unruly like I wanted her. Unkept. Rebellious. In need of discipline to a degree I saw fit. In time. Or not. Did it even matter anymore? It's not like I'd get in trouble. No one would ever know. But that wasn't who I was. It couldn't be. And then there was Porsha and the guilt. Maybe I just needed to throw myself in this slave and forget. Forget? No...*but yes.*

Fuck, I needed a drink. Something strong enough to drown out these conflicting thoughts. What a fucking mistake this all was. Nothing seemed right.

"Hurry and eat. I need to go out, and I'll have to chain you up. I don't have the patience to deal with any dramatics at the moment."

Small hands paused from whatever she was making on the counter. "You're leaving me here?"

"Not for long."

"I won't leave. I'll stay inside."

"Sure you will. I'm not risking it. Hurry up. I'm going to change out of this stupid suit." Even as I spoke, I was already heading to the room. The moment I broke the threshold of the closet, I stopped in my tracks. My head cocked to the side, and something told me to go back. Had I heard a sound? If she—

A prayer contorted with a wish until I wasn't sure what I was pleading for. Had I planned this all along?

I surged into the living room, cursing and growling as I raced to the door. It wasn't even shut all the way. As I entered the building's hallway, I saw her disappear around the side where the elevator was. Sprinting, I broke around the turn nearly colliding with a group of men who were waiting for the door to open. Red hair disappeared into the hallway going in the opposite direction and I had to give her props; she was fast. So much so, I pushed myself to speeds I hadn't reached since college. I was gaining on her, but not as much as I should have. Spirals swung over her shoulder as she spun back to look at me. The fear that locked with my gaze was exhilarating to the predator I kept hidden away inside. He awoke, thriving and forcing me faster as elation became all I knew. Fury wasn't even in the forefront anymore. Excitement. Lust. I could decimate this stupid girl if I wanted. Destroy her in ways that would traumatize her for life. She'd never be the same. I had that power, and it sent me to record-breaking speeds. I lunged, my hand thrusting as I grabbed a fistful of curls.

"No! No!" Screams left her, and doors opened. Any other day, I would have frozen in guilt. Internal alarms went off inside of me, but they only fed the beast who flourished in this public situation. Here, *she was mine*, whether I wanted her or not. Here...there was no reason for shame; quite the opposite. There were no rules concerning what was mine.

Foreign pleas mixed with phrases I could only assume were threats. Through her tone, her emotions spanned from scared to defensive. I didn't have to know her language to decipher that.

"If you don't want me to beat the ever-living hell out of you in front of everyone, I suggest you walk."

Keeping my hold to the hair at her scalp tight and high, I forced her forward while she continued to cry out. There was no way she could break free, and every time she tried to turn to me, I gave a hard shake, bringing more tears.

"Dear boy, I thought that was you. It's been years."

The voice leaving the inside of the elevator coming towards me was enough to bring my excitement to a crashing halt. Elec's words replayed in my mind, and I groaned, slowing, but not stopping.

"Master Sixty-three, is it?"

George Fredrick, doctor to the rich and famous—to my mother—my father, smiled. "You'd be correct. You?"

"Twelve-twelve. We should catch up. Right now isn't such a good time, but tomorrow find me."

"We'll do lunch. I'll contact you in the morning."

Nodding, I broke into the hall, my fake smile melting as I walked the two doors down, pushing the metal barrier opened with more force than I'd meant. With a shove, I sent the girl skidding across the wooden living room floor. Her mistake was not staying down. She was sobbing, screaming as she raced towards me. The adrenaline exploded back through, and I was ready. She was not.

W0023

Had I thought I'd escape while my new Master had least suspected it? Had I prayed I'd be able to find somewhere to hide until I came up with a plan? All my hope had been in the elevator door being opened when I made it that far. It hadn't been. Truthfully, I didn't even expect my Master to come looking for at least a few minutes after he changed, but he wasn't as distracted as I assumed. Nor as slow. For a girl, I could run faster than any Bordelli. That was saying a lot since there'd been eight who were within a few years of me. Here, I hadn't stood a chance. As I ran at him now, ready to risk my very life for freedom of any kind, even death, my Master was quick to show me I didn't stand a chance against him.

Screams were still leaving me, and I was swinging towards him as I approached. Had I at all been able to process that the man was smiling, I wouldn't have attacked at all, but I couldn't see anything but ending this now. It didn't happen as his arm shot down towards my hands making my body turn at the force. He gripped my hips and spun me for the back of the couch, ripping my shirt up, and pulling my panties off. The blow to my ass was so powerful, my head shot back, and I couldn't get enough air to suck in through my shock.

"Did I say I wanted a drink? I like your game a lot better, slave. Do you not see this was what I was trying to protect you from? I guess we're pulling off the band aid the first night. Why not."

My legs were kicking out and oxygen finally came, burning my lungs as I gulped in air. His hand came down over my ass again, and although I gasped and sobbed, I was still able to breathe.

"I don't want this. I want to go home."

"This is our home now, Clara. We don't have a choice."

Twisting, I threw my weight to the side, but my Master was ready. He let me step away from the couch, only to spin me back and pound his palm into my ass again. The pain was unreal, throbbing and burning my skin to a degree I'd never felt before. It almost brought me to my knees, but I fought harder. That brought me more crippling blows. I lost my breath repeatedly, choking on the sobs once they finally returned. His hand wrapped around my throat, squeezing as his palm once again connected. Oxygen wasn't my friend as I tried to break his suffocating hold. Between the pain and pressure against my neck, it evaded me. By the time it did return, stars danced in my vision, and I barely had the strength to keep fighting. He had to have sensed that. His hold eased, somehow jumpstarting me into action. I dove to the side, clawing into the leather sofa, managing to slide along the cushions until I was tumbling over the other side.

"If you run to that room, you condemn yourself. I wouldn't do it, slave. Walk around and face your punishment. If you do, I'll lock you up and we'll be done. If you continue this, you're going to hurt a lot more."

My voice was raw and raspy as I yelled out. "You *want* my pain."

"Damn right I do, but you're making a mistake in handing it over so freely. If you were smart, you'd spare yourself the discomfort and put a stop to it now. Walk back over here."

"The Bordelli are strong. We fight to the end."

"Idiot girl. So that's your decision? Run or fight?"

"I'm not a slave."

"You are. You're *my* slave, and before the morning comes, I will make you see that. Remember, whatever happens is your choice."

I rocked back and forth on my feet, not sure which way to go. I was beyond thinking with how this oil was making me feel. I was scared, angry, and turned on despite my behind being on fire. I needed the end of something. Whether it was this life or the fear, I had to keep going to find out. I wasn't raised to submit or bend to laws outside of our own. I sure as hell couldn't do that now.

"Where are you going, slave? You're not moving; are you done? Do you see the error of your ways? You can walk back and bend over."

My head shook.

"One."

The way his eyes watched me as he counted, he was ready. His gaze was eating me alive. My Master liked this.

"Two."

I started to inch left, watching him mirror me. I moved right, and so did he.

"Clara…"

Darting towards the room, I turned, throwing my weight into the door and feeling him crash into it before I could close it. I screamed, wedging my feet with the wall as I managed to hold him off from getting in. There were still a few inches before the barrier shut, but it wasn't opening anymore either.

Laughter. It joined in with my grunts as I gave it everything I had. One minute I was pushing, the next I was flying back at the crash. The door flew open, and I rolled, digging into the carpet as he jerked my ankle, pulling me. When he lifted and slammed me to the mattress, he didn't cover me with his weight as I expected, but he did climb on the bed. Instead, I was being flipped over on my stomach.

"I can't help but wonder if this is what you've really been waiting for. I saw your face when Elec forced you down. The way you increased your pain when I caught you and brought you here. You just can't stop yourself, can you? What does it do for you? Do you secretly like it? I want to see."

Buttons popped off at the pull of his shirt, and his knee was in my back as he took it off and began restraining my wrists with the material. The fire in my throat increased through my scream- ing, and I was trying to catch my breath from the heavy weight as he secured me and flipped me back over to face him. At the sight of him hovering over me shirtless, my voice caught in my throat. I was panting, even crying, but I wasn't jerking anymore.

I'd seen a few men shirtless during my life. My father. Rela- tives. People who were allowed into the caravan to help with services. Well, I only saw one of those shirtless, but I had been younger, and the stranger had gotten covered in mud to help us get unstuck. This man, this Master…he didn't look like them. He was all hard muscle and small circular scars. Seeing my Master shirtless was different. Forbidden, just like all the other nude slaves I had been surrounded by. All of this was not right, and yet I couldn't get over how my mind was having a hard time deciphering what I should feel.

"Why did you run to this room, Clara?"

He lowered the smallest amount, digging his fingers in hard to my inner thigh as he spread them. The pain should have broken the spell I was under, but all it did was drag me down deeper into the unknown. Into a part of myself I'd spent a life- time hiding away. How had he gotten all those scars? What was this sudden pressure of need making me move against the bed?

My skin was tingling. My head was beginning to shake back and forth for reasons that made no sense.

"I knew you were a fighter." Harder, his fingers squeezed into my flesh until my whimper couldn't be held. Tears spilled down my face, and I wasn't sure whether to keep fighting or see what happened. It could get worse either way. He wanted me to fight. I wanted to fight. The outcome wouldn't favor me if I chose to go that route, but I also couldn't give up now and just let him touch me. Dirty. It was all…wrong.

Twisting my hips to try to get away, my Master spread my legs even further apart. He slapped at my inner thigh with enough force to have me crying out. Oddly, it had me moving my hips to a sensation I didn't understand. My breaths were still labored, desperate, and for what, I didn't know. I hated this, but my body hadn't been my own since the oil was rubbed on me.

"Fuck. I don't even have to touch you to see how wet and swollen you are. God dammit. You're the dumbest girl alive. Beautiful, but so damn naïve."

"And you are a monster. Stop looking at me."

My accent was thick against my tongue as I tried to think outside of my language. Again, he savagely squeezed my thigh as I tried to shut my legs.

"*I own you.* I will look." His finger traced down my most private part, slapping over the sensitive nerves as a moan forcefully left me. "I will touch. I will taste." He sucked my juices from his fingertip, shocking me silent. "And I'm going to do with you what I want. It's that simple. You just figure out how you're going to accept all of that. Painfully…or…." *Slap!* "Painfully. I don't think either of us would have it any other way."

An aggravated sound left me as I rolled to my side. My legs coming together only trapped his hand deeper between my thighs, right to the one place I dared not touch. At least not up to this point. Before, privacy was not encouraged. I shared a small sleeping area with my brother and sisters. We females showered in the same area, but never together, just always taking turns. Complete isolation was few and far between. Not that I hadn't thought about this or how it would be when Donavon and I married. The curiosity was there, but I still wasn't sure what exactly to expect.

"No. You can't." Heat poured from me as he rolled me back to stare up at him, and again, he spread my legs. What was wrong with me? I had been manageable before, but now that his hands were all over me, so close to the ache I tried ignoring, I couldn't find the strength to physically fight to make him stop. Did I even want to anymore? I had no opinion. No thoughts other than the pleasure building as he traced the outsides of my folds.

"I can and will. You like this." His fingertip dipped into my entrance, and my eyes shot open. Not for long. They rolled back as I shook my head hard, trying to break myself from the spell. The action was my only denial. "Answer me. I want to hear you say it. I won't have you twisting this in the morning." His other hand lifted, and fingers pushed hard into my cheek with enough force to have my jaw separating. Pain webbed through my face and my small scream barely sounded like me at all. "Answer."

Still, he continued teasing me, waiting for me to respond. I didn't know how. I wasn't even sure what exactly was going on.

Slap.

The brief flare of pain over my private area had my head flying forward. My lids shot up, and I was on the edge of panic as something built deep inside me. There was such need. Such emptiness.

Slap.

Slap.

"This isn't...right. I'm wrong."

My Master's eyes narrowed through his confusion. I wasn't making sense, but my words were beyond this tsunami of sensation that was about to explode through me. I dropped my head and hair covered my face. I cried out as he slid his finger deeper inside of me.

"It has to be the fucking oil." My Master cursed. "It does this to you? It makes you want this?"

He stretched me further, sliding the other tip of his finger inside me. When he brushed his thumb over my clit, the burn was addicting. I almost started begging him for more. It was right on the tip of my tongue. So close all it would take was a word. But I wasn't there yet. Almost...but not quite.

MASTER B-1212

I should lock her up and leave now. Isn't that what my conscience was warning me to do? It was one thing to fight her into submission, something completely different to take advantage of her while she was drugged up. Not that I'd thought too much on it when I fucked Porsha on her pills. Still, hadn't that been a different situation entirely? Voluntary on Porsha's side? It was hard to say.

Too many questions kept barraging me. Morality and the lack thereof waged a war. How could I say I owned her, that I could do whatever I want to her, and then go back on my word as if I hadn't said it. I had. She was a slave, and in that moment I sure as fuck had every intention of treating her as one. I still did, and that was the biggest war I was facing. I was a Master here. If I wanted to leave, I had to accept this. The fact that I was even arguing with myself internally had to count for something, right?

"Clara, what do you feel?"

Such a ridiculous question. I could clearly see. If I only knew how the oil worked, maybe it would have helped to gage her mindset. She either wanted this or not, but could I believe any answer she gave me? Surely it wouldn't interfere with her truth. It sedated; it didn't alter her fucking mind.

Would it matter if it did?

"You have to speak. Your body may be close to release, but what about you? *Answer me*, slave. Do you like this?"

The silence had me removing my fingers to slap against her pussy again. She jumped, moaning out. Her face grew even more flushed as she writhed below me. If she wouldn't have been a virgin, maybe I would have already fucked her on the spot. Thing was, I had no idea who she'd turn into once my cock got inside her. The pain could trigger another episode. One I wanted even more by the second. I'd never had a virgin before…but I sure as fuck did right now.

Bringing my palm down hard over one inner thigh and then the other, Clara went back to sobbing and trying to press her legs together. She didn't scatter or try escaping. She was dealing with the pain, even when I hit her harder than I should. Thing was, I had to gauge her threshold. More importantly…I was curious to see how far I would go without consequences. Death didn't interest me, but…no worries. No limits. I did like that.

"Make it stop. Make it—"

She gasped as I leaned over, bringing my hand back to cup her pussy. Her hips arched and she let out a cry as I rubbed through her juices, easing two fingers in deep. When I hit the wall of her virginity, I cursed, more in agony for my hard cock than the annoyance of the wall I was going to break through.

Blood.

Hers would be on me by the time I was done. She'd be truly mine when she'd been meant to marry another man. Why that was so satisfying, I had no idea. It had never appealed before, yet now, in this moment as I watched her beautiful features tightened with her approaching orgasm, I felt the power the entire situation held. He'd be looking for his pretty little virgin. Mourning her disappearance…and she'd be here, fucking me. Crying out and moaning *for me*, her Master.

I liked it.

"You want me to make it stop?"

I tugged at my belt, jerking open my pants as her lids squeezed shut. I took them off, still waiting for her to come more to her senses. The slave's legs were spreading while the hands restrained underneath her were fisted so tight the digits were almost white as they held to the blanket.

"Master. What is this…happening? It won't…stop. I can't." Her legs kicked out around me, only to draw up closer to her body. When my finger lightly circled her clit, an agonizing sound filled the space with her plea. "Master?"

Vibrant green met me. As Clara took in my undressed frame, she sobbed, rocking her hips. I grabbed my cock, levelling it at her entrance. Easing the tip inside, I stroked my length, testing how it'd even feel to be inside of her. My slave pushed down, crying out as I bit my teeth into each other at the tightness. My head still wasn't completely inside of her, but that's as far as I could get. One small push forward and I'd hit the wall marking her virginity. I was so tense; I was almost content to just stay here as I continued stroking myself. It was hot keeping that piece of her intact. I could still come in her. Just like this. I could even watch cum shoot right into what was mine if I pulled back enough.

The possibilities ranged as she moved against me. She was so close, trying to ride me, wanting more. She liked it, and so did I, but like always, pleasure wasn't enough. Instinct had me sitting back and wrapping my hand around the side of her neck as I caressed the front with my thumb. I eased in even more, securing my grip, using it to bring her down to the point the wall stopped me. Clara jolted in pain at the contact, and her eyes met mine. She didn't thrash or fight as she kept moving, needing more to push her over the edge.

"Fuck, this pussy is good." I brought my weight forward, watching her eyes flare at the shift of my hand. It completely covered the front of her throat. I gripped, testing my strength against the delicate area. "I could get used to this, slave. You put up a good fight, but it isn't over yet." I used my other hand to tease her clit while I continued to let her control the rocking.

"This is bad. Es…" Another whimper as the two languages collided. "It's not coming. I can't."

"Because I don't want you to yet. Do you play with yourself a lot?"

I increased the motion over the sensitive nub until tears were leaving her again. When she didn't answer, I squeezed her throat making her go wild as I took away her ability to breathe. Legs shifted and tried kicking against me, and her head went back and forth as she attempted scooting away from me at the same time. With my hold locked on, she didn't stand a chance. Mass shades of red darkened, and I only let go when her fight began to ease from impending unconsciousness.

Clara gasped, sucking in air but coughing.

"When I ask you a question, you answer."

"N-Never. I never play."

"Never?"

"Dirty."

"Not once?"

Still, she kept inhaling deeply as I kept my hold steady.

"You've come though, right?"

At her confusion, something twisted in my brain. Had I thought she was innocent before? So many ideas collided at the possibilities I began seeing with this slave.

"Clara, the feel-good feeling. Orgasms. You've had them before, haven't you?"

She gasped as I pinched to the top of her folds, teasing her clit without so much stimulation. When I let go of her throat to tease her breast, she cried out even louder.

"Once. In a dream, I think. I...need. We shouldn't," she sobbed, "talk about this. *I can't.*"

"You'll talk to me about whatever I want. You'll talk, you'll come. Baby, I'm going to make you scream so good. To feel good though, it's going to hurt. You know this?"

Her fearful eyes searched mine. She truly was clueless, only adding to the racing in my mind. Clara was completely innocent. A virgin yes, but an untainted one. I could make her believe anything. I could make her like what I did. I could corrupt her pleasure, bending it to my own needs, and she'd never know the difference.

Manipulation...Malevolence...

"Do you feel this?" I moved my hips, withdrawing from her, only to push my head back in. Clara moaned, nodding desperately as the oil calmed her again. She was trying to rock, trying to keep the pleasure going. "I have a lot to go to be inside of you all the way. That's where it feels really good, but to do that," I nudged into the wall of her virginity, making her jump and cry out. "I have to get through that. I'm leaving the choice to you. Do you want to keep doing this, or do you want to take a little pain to make it feel really good?"

"I..."

While she thought, I got lost in the way her pussy kept clenching around me. With the pad of my thumb, I dipped down, tracing her folds that were to each side of my width. I stroked down my length, using my head to make a path all over her slit. I took my time, not forcing an answer one way or another. She'd decide this. I was going to come in her regardless. *How deep, was the question.*

"Master."

I glanced to her face for the first time in minutes. Red was rosy on her cheeks as her glazed eyes were nearly hidden by heavy lids. She licked her lips, and I noticed how swollen they were as she continuously pressed them into each other. I'd never wanted to kiss lips so much in my life. Kiss. Bite. Suck. *Choke.* Her beauty had quadrupled when she was wearing the pleasure I brought her. It was almost too much, like a dream.

"Have you decided between this or the pain?"

"You can make this feeling stop?"

"I can, but only if from here on out you're good. No more running. If you stay, I'll keep this feeling away. Otherwise, I'll oil you up every day and let you suffer just like this from here on out."

Horror. She even sobbed at my words.

"No more oil. I can't bear it. I'll stay; I'm Bordelli. I'm strong. I choose the pain."

I nodded, moving back to put myself over her. Lowering, I let our lips brush. At first, Clara didn't know what to do, but she quickly caught on, letting her tongue come out to meet mine as I traced it over her lips. She rocked, and I reached under her, tugging at my shirt to release her hands. A wince and sound poured into my mouth as she battled the feeling returning to them. Within minutes, our kissing became more passionate. She held around me, tightening her grip and moving against the tip I had eased into her. I withdrew, starting my motions slow, barely even inside. In. Out. In. Out.

"Just like that," I whispered to her lips. "Move that pussy against me. Feels good, right?"

"Yes." She brought her legs up higher.

In.

Out.

In.

"You're so beautiful. Eyes red from crying. Lips swollen but wanting more. Feel me. Think how much you're going to like it when I'm deeper inside you, making you feel better than you ever have. I can do that for you, slave. You're going to love this when the pain passes."

In.

Out.

With each thrust, my need to make her scream was torture. It all rested on me, and I was the one in control. I could make it happen at any time. She'd be surprised, oblivious to what was coming, and I loved that the most.

In.

Out.

I brought one of my hands to the side of her bruised throat, keeping the placement as I soaked in her pulse.

Thump-thump.

Thump-thump.

It was strong. Steady.

"Hold to me, Clara. Know this is all going to be worth it. I'll have you coming all over my cock in no time."

I met her lips, barely finishing before surging through the barrier. A scream filled my mouth as I kissed her hard, holding myself still as I tightened on her neck. *Thump-thump-thump-thump.* It was hammering now. Pounding against my fingers from her pain and fear. I could have come on the spot for the completion and victory my darkness felt. A sob vibrated my lips, and she sniffled as I withdrew, pushing into her deeper. The gasp had her eyes shooting right to mine. I kissed her again, withdrawing and letting her test the sensations as I started the slow thrusts.

"Do you feel it changing, slave?"

At the pause and continued cries, my hold tightened on her throat causing her lids to fly open. I didn't miss the small dots of broken blood vessels in her eyes. And like I knew, fear that I would choke her again like before, had her head quickly nodding.

"It's...better."

"Just wait."

My satisfaction surged, and I reached down with my other hand, right back to her clit so I could build her up all over again.

It didn't take long before she was moving against me again, whimpering and shifting her hips with the thrusts. "Time to go deeper and make you feel really good."

But it was already feeling good for her. I could tell by the way she clung to my neck. With how much louder her moans were already turning. Had she not been on the oil, I didn't think she would have bounced back so fast, but here, she was desperate. She needed my cock, and I was about to merge her learning experience with the only way I enjoyed this.

My fingers dug into her ass as I reached under, holding to her as I buried myself. I ground my weight forward, increasing the hold as Clara's pleasure morphed with the pain as I squeezed harder than I'd ever allowed myself. She moaned; she cried out, trying to wiggle away from the agony. She was trapped in her own battle, and it showed as Clara sunk her teeth into my shoulder. My own discomfort was so unexpected, maybe I would have reacted had she not immediately stopped. She hadn't done it as an attack, but a reaction as she moved faster against me. I shifted, pushing to sit as both my hands locked around her neck. Had she not been so close, perhaps fear would have caused her to react in panic. Thing was, Clara was starting to scream, tightening and spasming around my cock as I beat it into her mercilessly. Blood coated my length, and I stared down in fascination at what I'd taken. At what I'd done. From the darkening marks on her face to her throat, to her hips, thighs, and the bruises I knew were covering her ass. My sins were evident for all to see, and there was nothing anyone could do about it. They wouldn't care to.

To make it better...She'd been a virgin. Pure. Mine to fuck up however I wanted, if I chose to. Teach. Train. Something happened to me in that moment, and I couldn't begin to understand it as I stared at her in awe, but I liked it. I needed it. *Needed this.*

My cock thickened, pulling me from the deep recesses of my

sick mind. That I was on the brink of my own orgasm was shocking. My gaze broke from the blood, and I glanced back to my slave. She was blissful, riding the high after her orgasm. My grip increased even more on her throat, and I let a growl tear free, squeezing enough to show her who was in control. I held her life. I was in charge of her pleasure, pain, and how much of it I'd allow her to experience.

"Keep your eyes on me, slave. Don't you dare fucking look away."

Hands shot to my wrists, and I let my stare penetrate hers. I let her feel what was inside of me, allowing time to drag out through her shallow breaths. This was the beginning. A taste at what I knew would get worse. Outside of this, I was social. Nice. Easygoing. But this part of me I hid here, inside, was... becoming accustomed. Watching. *Growing.* With the truth so visible between us, I let my cum fill what I now owned. Into Clara. Into my slave.

W0023

"Alright, you've showered, you've eaten, and you've gone to the restroom. I'm leaving. The TV is on, I'll be back in an hour or two. Be good."

I rolled my eyes, taking in the large screen with people cooking. I'd seen televisions before throughout my life. I'd even caught a few shows from time to time when I snuck into the laundry mat a few blocks from where we stayed, but I'd never gotten to relax enough to enjoy anything. I wasn't even technically supposed to watch them given the dirty content most played, but after the night I had, I wasn't going to judge a tv show.

"Slave, did you hear me?

"Maybe the slave heard. Me, Clara, didn't care to hear. Are you going? *I'm busy.*"

"Keep running your mouth and throwing your fit, but know when I get back, I'm taking you again."

I wouldn't even look at the smirk I knew was on his face. "Dirty. Are you still here?"

"Yes, but I'll be back. Be ready for me. This time I'm going to—"

"Ugh, you want me sick! Go before you condemn us both."

"Be ready."

My anger couldn't be hidden as I refused to give him my attention. Laughter filled the room and I glanced over, watching as he waved his hand towards me in dismissal and disappeared from the bedroom. Why was my body already on fire again just from him saying that? I shouldn't want to experience having him inside me again. I had enough bruises to last me a lifetime. My body didn't care. The oil was still in me, or what it had done was. Maybe it was a brain sickness, and I'd never stop thinking forbidden thoughts.

"Bye, my beautiful slave!"

"Leave me!" Curse words in my language poured through the small apartment. It had him laughing again. The door shut and I couldn't hold to the aggravation or anger when I should have. Had I really let him do that to me last night? Was I so weak to not fight the effects of the oil? My body said I wasn't weak. I was sore in places I'd never been before, but it was a good sore. An arousal sore. I wouldn't think about how scratchy my throat sounded, or how much it hurt to swallow. I refused to look at my eyes in the mirror. No...not even how it hurt to move. None of that compared to the dirty acts I'd enjoyed or how enticing it was to feel it again.

Clinking rattled against metal as I shifted my arm. I winced through the jolt of pain, laying down. I had a good amount of leeway to move, but I still couldn't escape the one cuff if I wanted to. I didn't even bother to try as I turned off the television. Had I even slept? My Master was ravenous when it came to having me. Once. Twice. I'd only just fallen asleep in the early morning when he decided to have me again. Or maybe that one had been my fault. No wonder my Master was in a good mood. Now he spoke of a fourth?

Yawning, I snuggled to the pillow, closing my eyes. Colors warped, weaving and fading. For the smallest moment I was by the bonfire again. It was night and my father played the guitar as my mother sang with the other women. There was such happiness at the upcoming marriage of me and Donavon. I could still see his smile as he stared across the fire at me. His sandy blond hair was almost to his wide shoulders and the dirt was still covering his shirt from the hard labor of clearing the adjoining field for the O'Farrill's who were letting us stay on their property for the cost of labor. The night had been perfect. Then...I'd had to go to the bathroom. The walk wasn't far away. It was one I had to have done a hundred times in the last few weeks. The night was darker than normal, and I'd never seen the man who stood in the shadows. He was there...and then something over my face and mouth, and more dark.

"What did I tell you. She's beautiful, isn't she? I saw her on my day off, on the way to pick up more supplies. She's going to make me a lot of money."

That had been the beginning of my journey to this place. It was a memory I hadn't thought of in months. One so painful, it only found me in the realm of dreams.

"Slave. Clara."

I jumped at the hand on my bicep, blinking the dark room I'd been kept in away. Had I known how lucky I was now, I'd be thanking the Gods those two men had kept their hands off me until I arrived here.

"Whoa. Shh. It's okay." Brown eyes scanned over my face as I pushed to sit. He'd already uncuffed me, and I rolled my wrist through the stiffness.

"You're here."

At my dry tone, he smiled. "I told you I'd return. And what did I say when I left?" He pulled my hips, sliding me so I returned to my back. "I said be ready."

"Impossible. I hurt. You broke me there. Later. I need food."

A seriousness swept his features. "Shit, I forgot." His head lowered. "I promised Sixty-three we'd have lunch with him and his slave." Glancing at his watch, he groaned. "We have a little time. Not much. Elec kept me later than I thought.

"It's early. You smell like papa. Vodka. Where's mine."

"Ha! You're good. Be better and spread your legs."

At the sting to my skin from his slap, I sucked in air, glaring in his direction. It only had him smiling bigger. He wanted me to fight. Instead, I spread as wide as I could, turning my face away.

"Make it fast. I need food."

Whack!

"Ze vouch."

"What the hell is that?" My Master flipped me to my stomach, spreading my legs as he removed his pants.

"It's pig fucker."

Whack!

My legs drew in and to the side at the explosion, and my sob was immediate.

"Pig fucker. Original. I'm guessing that's a really bad word given your constant worry about filth. So, you think I'm dirty?"

"Do you think you're not? Look at what you do."

He righted me and pried my legs apart, fitting himself between them as he started rubbing along my slit. "I don't think this is dirty. I think it's clean. I bathed it myself. And being as I'm about to be fucking you, I wouldn't consider you a pig."

I glared over my shoulder, crying out as he fisted my hair, pulling my head back. Lips brushed gently over mine, cradling under my chin as he held me as far as my head would go.

"I'm tempted to cancel lunch. I don't think you deserve to go out anyway. You're a bad slave. You don't know how to behave. You'd do nothing but cause trouble and add to the headache I'm already starting to get. Besides, you wouldn't want a friend. That's what Sixty-three is looking for, a friend for his slave. He adores her, and supposedly she's so well behaved. A good slave. Not like you."

"*I am good.* I am better than this slave."

47

"Yeah right. You're horrible. You can't even take a cock without crying about it."

At my anger, my accent thickened.

"Because it's a big cock. Es too big. Off with you. I am not bad."

He let go, sitting and jerking up my hips. "On your knees. Keep your head on the bed.

"I'm good and not a slave. I'm Clara, and I'm good."

At wetness from his pre-cum sliding over my folds, my head jerked up. *Whack!* The spanking brought more tears.

"I said, *down.* I thought you said you were good."

An aggravated sound left me as I dropped it back to the pillow. "I'm better than this slave. Why do you do that? Tease?"

"Are you not getting turned on? You like this."

The head of his cock explored around my entrance, moving towards my clit. The sensations were so strong, I found myself pushing back against him as he nudged inside, only to continue rubbing over me. For minutes he built me up, introducing me into something so wicked I was sure I'd bring every plague against me for the amount I enjoyed it.

"Lean." He lifted my ass higher. "Keep yourself like this. You'll learn. Sixty-three's slave was a d[1]. Docile and trained. Elec tells me she's really sweet and completely embraces her status. She was in school to be a therapist before she was taken. I guess she was allowed to help transition girls into this life before she even went to auction. Our Main Master is thinking about letting her continue with her duties to the new slaves brought in. Not only that, George tells me she follows a schedule he made. While I was tossing shots this morning thinking about what to do with you and your attitude, she was making him breakfast and coffee. Maybe I should have gotten me a d, too. I bet you can't even cook."

"I'll burn your food on purpose talking like that. Cook for you, noy. *You cook for me now.*"

The bed shook with his laughter. I didn't find it funny. I could cook. I was a fantastic cook. And I was good. My mother taught me all things.

"I bet she can't make clothes or breadska from scratch. I can."

"Breadska?"

"Sweet bread. Special bread. I'll make and you'll see. Coffee. Ha. More like dirty water. She doesn't know anything about coffee. I'll make it right, the Bordelli way. You'll like it; you'll see."

"Someone's all fired up."

He tapped his tip against my clit again, stopping my rant in its tracks. A sigh left me, and I let myself get lost in the need.

"Are you done?"

I moaned, content to lose myself in the pleasure.

"I take that as a yes."

"I'm done."

"Good."

The bed shifted and teeth bit into my ass sending me stiffening and yelping. As soon as I thought I could enjoy, he stole it, transitioning it to something new. In an odd way, *better*. Nails raked down my back as he repositioned himself on his knees.

"Do you remember what I said last night?"

"No pleasure without pain."

"Yes."

Pressure fit against my opening. The stinging was back and had me gripping to the sheet that covered the mattress. In. Out. He eased his cock in, careful not to do more damage than he'd already done. I was so sore, yet he kept getting it to feel good.

"I love these hips and thighs." He held tightly, sliding inside me even more. I went to lift when he pushed me back down. "Be good like you say you are. Take it, slave. It's not too big for you."

Something wet rolled down my back causing me to turn my

head to the other side to try to see. I couldn't, but what I could do was feel, and it didn't take long before my mind started to get fuzzy. Thoughts faded, but I knew this need suddenly taking over me. I was getting soaking wet, moaning and cursing at the same time.

"The Main Master gave you that oil? But you said—"

"You let me worry about what I said. I know what I'm doing, slave. You'll come and it'll relax you. I need you good at lunch."

"How can I be good with the oil? You know how it makes me. You're a cruel Master."

"Bet your ass I am, but I don't care. I'm so fucking hot for you. You're going to be hot for me too. While we're there, you're going to be thinking about me sucking and fucking this pussy." His thrust increased, bringing me higher and higher with every slam he made into me.

"But I won't be able to focus."

"You will because I say you will. Listen to me. You're going to be better than her, aren't you Clara? Prettier. Nicer. You have that aura. You project the royalty you are, and you're going to do that during lunch, aren't you? You'll make me look good. Together, we'll be better than everyone. A powerful Master and his obedient, gorgeous, perfect slave. Sort of like a First Lady or queen. That's you."

My head lifted as I arched even more.

"I want to hear you agree." His hand locked painfully around the back of my neck, forcing me down. "Say you're going to be good. You have one chance to prove it to me. If you ruin this, you'll never leave this apartment again."

"I'm better than good. I am Bordelli."

His fingers slid to my hair, tightening the curls in his fist until I was crying out. "Don't twist my words and pretend not to know what I mean. You are good, but you'll behave good as well."

"I'll be good. I'll…"

Pulling me to sit up, he barred his hold over my waist so that he was buried in me. With his arm locked to my throat, his forearm stayed pressed between my breasts. I was right there as he held me still. My orgasm was on the brink while he kept me waiting with the pulsing of his fingers on my neck. It was a threat. A wish.

"Say it all together. I'll be on my best behavior, Master."

"I'll be…" my mouth shot open as his other arm lifted and he began teasing the sensitive nerves, rubbing over the top of my slit. Slow. More. Faster. I could feel his cock jerk inside. Feel how close he was as I clutched around him. "I'll be on my best behavior, Master. I'll be perfect. Good. *Please.*"

He pushed my head back to the bed, holding it down as he pounded into me. I screamed, not able to move as he fucked me to the point where I could barely catch my breath. It didn't help when his palm exploded over my ass and thighs, repeatedly. When he pulled out, I felt warmth from his cum shoot all over the throbbing flesh. My weight fell to the side, only for him to catch me and ease me to my stomach as he climbed off.

"Pitiful, slave. You'll learn to hang. If not, I guess I can always trade you in for a d^2."

MASTER B-1212

"Oh, so close. Here, like this. Let me show you."

Emerald eyes narrowed at the next table, disappearing under aggravated lids, only to relax, focus…and repeat. She was working so hard on folding the napkin into a boat like slave d[1], but she wasn't having much luck. Seeing the two girls talk and spend time together shouldn't have amused me as much as it did, but my slave was a spitfire. She was loud, bratty, and very much didn't want to give credit where it was due. But she was caring, observant, and deep down under all that fire, strong. She'd been bred to lead her group by marrying into their main line. By calling her a bad slave, I knew she would want to prove she wasn't. It was the oldest trick in the book, and she'd fallen for it. That went to show how gullible she was. How pure and innocent. There was something special about that that I liked.

"I had no idea I'd see you down here. Have you been part of this life for long?"

George Fredricks laughed. "No, not long at all. I'd been accepted into Whitlock shortly before it fell. I never even got to attend an auction because of how that went down. It was pretty wild, but then I suddenly got a call to meet about this place. I jumped at the opportunity. I mean," he gestured to the women. "We can't have this life up there. Not that what I do is all that bad, it's just…no one understands us like our slaves. It's nice to have this environment to escape to."

I found myself nodding for reasons I wouldn't have understood yesterday. Ones I was still trying to process right now as I took in Clara's flushed cheeks. Never in a million years had I ever imagined drugging anyone, yet here I was, keeping my slave oiled up for my convenience. Not that I planned to do that all the time like other Masters, but I was already seeing a difference in myself, and it was happening fast.

"I'm glad you invited us to lunch. I wasn't sure I'd be able to get my slave to behave well enough out in public, but I was wrong. She's learning quickly. Having a friend for her could be a good thing. Especially when we're gone. I mean, Elec told me earlier the slaves just live here, as we do up there. They can order their groceries to be delivered or pick them up themselves. They can shop, go to movies. They live their lives here and just wait for us to return. I feel better leaving, knowing she has a friend."

"Exactly. I feel the same. It's good for them to have someone to rely on when we're away. Say, how long will you be staying?"

I shrugged, my lips twisting. "Until Elec and my father decide I've accepted who I am. I have no idea how long that could take. I sure as hell haven't held back so it's not like I'm not trying to embrace this. I am doing a lot better than I thought I would, that's for damn sure."

A smile tugged at my lips as Clara's eyes shot open and she laughed, holding up her boat from the next table so I could see. Excitement, it was clear as her stare stayed on me and she licked her lips. She shifted in her seat, tearing her gaze from mine as she went back to talking. Had she not been on the oil, I wasn't sure how she'd behave. Fine, was my guess, but it was debatable. I didn't like that. She needed to accept this without having to be calmed. Hadn't Elec said most slaves had been here for months. Acceptance wouldn't be hard if she felt safe. The need to not be able to escape was already programmed in. Out here, there was even more freedom. That had to count for something.

"Maybe you'll be here only another week or two until the drama up there fades."

"You heard about that?"

At my deepening tone, he shrugged. "I'm afraid with my job, I'm brought in for a lot of things, especially concerning politics. Most take care of business while I go through our appointments. It's not like a doctor's office where they come to me. I fit into their lives. I see and hear a lot."

"I bet you do. I didn't kill her," I assured. "Porsha popped pills. She was an addict and depressed. She was in a bad place long before she got to the point of suicide. I just…I was with her two nights before she took her life, and there was evidence of that."

"Bruising. *A lot.* Just like with your slave." He paused. "I saw the morning of the auction. Your father brought me in as a precaution to look at the autopsy pictures to see what I thought."

"Fuck. Of course he did."

"He covers all bases. I assured him your marks had nothing to do with her death."

"I told him that. He didn't believe me."

Master Sixty-three shrugged. "I'm sure he called someone after me too. Your father doesn't usually take one person's word about it. Give it time. This will pass. Then, you can come here and completely forget the worries of that world. Your slave, she's pretty. You seem to like her well enough."

The rosiness on Clara's cheeks kept sucking me in. She really was beautiful when she smiled and laughed. For the smallest moment, I even forgot she was a slave. She was dressed like any normal woman out for lunch: a mauve-colored sundress with a jean jacket, a thin, gold necklace she'd found in a small jewelry box in the closet, sandals. Hell, she'd even tested out some mascara and lip gloss she'd found in a makeup bag in our bathroom. Her wild hair bounced at every move, and I was mesmerized by her. Especially since she was covered in my bruises. She even seemed to not be bothered by them. Had I met her on the outside world...

"She's okay. We're in a trial phase. I'll see how she works out. So far, so good. She's a lot better than last night so that makes me happy."

The doctor forced a smile. "You did seem to have your hands full. I'm glad you've turned her around this morning. You know," his voice dropped as he leaned in closer. "If for some reason she doesn't get better, I could always get you something to keep her calm. The Gardens offer something close, but their oil or medication doesn't always have the desired side effects we sometimes need. I have connections that could get me anything on the market, right under the table. Slip it in her food, rub it on her as a cream, give it to her as a shot. There are so many options, and she might thank you for it in the end."

Easing back, I let my head shake despite I wanted to strangle him. Had he not heard anything about the events I was just faced with? The oil was one thing; it was a sedative that brought on lust. Elec said it wasn't addicting. That had been my biggest concern. The last thing I needed was another fucking Porsha.

"Thank you, but I'd like to see how this goes before I take that route. It's kind of you to offer though."

"Any time, just give me a call." He glanced at the women, his lips parting, only to clamp shut. "I really should be getting back though. It's almost time for mine's medication, and I'm afraid she's on a schedule. It was great meeting with you. Let's do this again tomorrow."

"Clara would like that. You got it."

I took in the girls giggling. Master Sixty-three's slave was leaned in whispering something that obviously made Clara laugh. When George approached, the slave stood, saying her goodbyes. Clara immediately came to sit across from me where George had been. She popped a candy in her mouth, her eyes dazzling.

"I was good."

"Yes, slave, I'm impressed and really proud of you. Not one outburst on your part." I took a drink of my water. "How do you feel?"

She rocked on the booth, wiggling just the smallest amount.

"Tired, a little, but I like this."

"Me too. What do you say we go the long route through the orchard on our way back? Then, we can catch a nap."

Clara did something between a moan and a squeal. "I'd like that a lot. Can I take my shoes off in the field? I want to feel the earth. Can I have it?"

"Have what? Dirt?"

"Yes, on my feet."

"Sure." I stood, shrugging. "For someone who doesn't like filth, you want your feet in the dirt? Amazing. I don't get you, slave. I'm trying, but I'm at a loss."

"Come. The earth is good. You'll like it."

"Me?"

I let her drag me out onto the busy main street. For long moments we could hardly move, but when we finally broke to the side road, we were able to actually go a steady pace.

"There, the trees, *come*."

Clara dragged me as she practically ran. I was jogging and laughing as she let go and took off her sandals. She was a free spirit through and through, and I hadn't got to witness many of those. Porsha had been in our youth, but it just wasn't in the times anymore. Life made us lost. Busy. We thrived to work. We never played or connected anymore.

"Yes. This is what we need. Heaven. Master, che-bah. Shoes, hurry, take them off. Feel this."

A groan left me as I glanced around. No one was near us or the empty stage not far away. I leaned down, taking off my shoes and socks to step into the grass. Why, I had no fucking idea. This was ridiculous. Still, I went through it if it meant she'd be good and happy. After all, she might not be after I introduced my knife. Nothing big, but...satisfying.

"There. Better?"

I picked up my shoes in time for her to grab my free hand and pull me deeper into the apple trees. The more under the canopy we got, the darker it became.

"We should bring a basket next time. I'll make colpa for you."

"Colpa? What is that?" I looked at all the apples. "Applesauce, or do you mean pie?"

"Yes, pie! Faster," she laughed.

"I think I gave you too much oil. Where are we going?"

Clara slowed, letting her shoes fall to the ground as she threw her arms around my neck. This was not the same woman I bought at the auction. There was no way. Elec said just a small swipe. There was nothing small about what I did across her back. Fuck. Not that I was complaining at her pulling at my zipper. Still, I'd have to be careful with how much I gave her. The longer the doctor's words sat in my mind, the more I was starting to think about giving my slave anything. I couldn't get her used to being like this. Not if I wanted to save myself one hell of a headache in the future.

"Hey." I stopped her hands making nearly blacked-out emerald eyes shoot up to mine. She was breathing hard, almost transfixed to what she'd been trying to do. And she was shaking, trembling as she let go. Her face appeared to be getting pale, but I wasn't sure in the dimness. "Back at home. Let's walk, okay? No rush."

"Oh." She swallowed hard, nodding, almost seeming lost for the briefest moment. Yes, this wasn't my slave right now. Every second that went by she seemed to be even more out of it. "Master...I...don't feel very good."

"I know. I'm sorry. I think that's my fault. Here, let's get you home."

My arm wrapped around her, pulling her in close as she gagged. Once. Twice. But nothing came up. I led us to the light in the far distance, watching to make sure she didn't become sick. The orchard wasn't extremely large, but it was a generous size. When Clara began to stumble, I had no other choice but to scoop her into my arms. She could barely stand anymore as she clutched her shoes and tiny purse to her chest.

"Slave, talk to me. You're not going to be sick, are you?" But she could barely hold her eyes open. Had I fucked her up so much with the oil? She wasn't even writhing or doing anything sexual anymore. She was just dead weight in my arms as she tried to look at me. "Clara."

My steps grew faster, moving to a light jog until I was reentering the light of the city. We were at the far end now, close to the main gate. I headed for the elevator, scanning one of the signs. Pounding thudded in my chest, beating against me so hard that I could barely stop pressing the damn button for the elevator. When it opened, I lunged on, once again hitting the hospital's level on the third floor.

"Clara." I growled through my fear as a Master and slave gave me more space. She was so pale. Her eyes rolled, but she was beyond consciousness, and it made my stomach twist and tear as guilt washed away any shadowing status as a Master I had. I wasn't without empathy. I felt something, and fault pulled in all the blame I harbored concerning Porsha. Maybe on some level I killed her, but that was questionable. Here...I was every bit responsible for my slave's condition.

"Move." The order boomed from my voice as the door opened and people began to try to crowd on. I ran forward, not caring that my shoes had fallen from my fingertips at the bump against another Master. I turned, pushing with my back to open the glass doors that enclosed the hospital. "Hey, you! I need some help."

People looked up from the front desk, but my eyes were on the white coat that had been looking over paperwork. He was already rushing towards me. From his stare, I knew he recognized me, but I didn't fucking care. I would not be responsible for killing my slave. I would not add another number unintentionally to my list of dead fucking lovers.

"What happened?"

Hands grabbed at her, but I couldn't let go as he rushed us into a room not feet away. I sat Clara on the bed, only giving the doctor just enough room to start checking her eyes with the light.

"I don't know. I mean, we were fine and she just...I gave her oil earlier. About two hours or so ago. She was fine. We had lunch. We socialized, then, this. It happened so fast."

"Oil? From here?"

"Yes, the fucking oil. The one to calm the slaves. Could I have given her too much? Did I...?"

The doctor barked orders as nurses began filling the room.

"Master, you need to give us space. We need you to go to the front and fill out the required paperwork."

"Like hell—"

"Master." The doctor's eyes narrowed with his own authority. "I am in charge here. Go. I'll let you know what's happening when I figure it out myself.

WOO23

"*Overdose? You said it was fine. I didn't fucking do this intentionally, Elec. You didn't warn me what would happen if I put too much. How the fuck was I supposed to know I'd almost kill her?*"

"*Calm down, Rob. She's fine.*"

"*She's not. Do you fucking see my slave?*

"*It wasn't the oil. It couldn't have been, we've checked it thoroughly. I've even had slaves bathed in that stuff and not once did any have a reaction like this. We'll get to the bottom of it, okay? I have every test available being run on what was in her system. If it exists, we'll find it.*"

I tried blinking, moving, anything but laying here unresponsive, but darkness was all I saw. It was so heavy against me, pulling me back down to the root of the real issue. Hadn't I known this was going to happen? Hadn't I welcomed it with open arms after my behavior? I'd been ready to give in to my Master. I had wanted him right there in that apple orchard as I was beginning to get sick, and my God knew that. He knew and was punishing me at my evil, dirty ways.

"I don't like the way you're looking at me, Elec. I didn't do this."

"I'm not saying you did."

"But I see what you're thinking. Porsha, now Clara."

"Clara? You call her by her real name?"

"Are you listening to me? I didn't do this. I'm not poisoning these women."

"I'm not saying you are. I truly wouldn't care if you did. It's your slave. You can do with her what you like."

"Do you not see the bruises on her neck. Her arms? All over her? Look. Look at her. I did that. I admit it. This, I did not do."

"Calm, Rob. You're getting too worked up. I told you I didn't think you did. We'll figure this out. You're upset, and after what you've been through, you have every right to be. Let's go grab some coffee. It's nearly been twenty hours. Maybe she'll wake up soon."

But I wasn't sure I wanted to. This wasn't my Master's fault, it was mine. I did this. I invited the illness the moment I didn't fight back. I was meant for another man. Promised to him. It didn't matter that I'd never see Donavon again. I hadn't taken vows but that obviously was irrelevant. I was betrothed, despite not wanting to be, and here I was paying for going back on my word.

I gave into the darkness again, refusing to fight my fate as I took the punishment. Voices came and went. Pressure from hands touched me and disappeared. Time. It went by in a blur of nightmares I didn't want to remember.

"I brought shoes and clothes. I figured since you wouldn't leave, you could at least shower and change here. I can't stand your walking around everywhere without shoes. If—"

"Hold on, Elec. Clara? She's moving her fingers. Slave, can you hear me?"

"Nothing. She's still out. Rob, go shower. I'll stay and watch over her until you finish."

61

It was as if seconds only passed before light flooded in. I blinked, squinting as a familiar face came into view. Water was going on in the background, and I couldn't get my thoughts to process as I stared into Elec's face. His eyes were inquisitive. Curious. I cleared my throat as he held a glass forward. I took a sip from the straw, scanning the room for where I even was. Slivers of something returned, but I couldn't understand what it was.

"How do you feel?"

"Where?" I cleared my throat. "Where am I?"

"The hospital. Seems you were poisoned."

"Poisoned?" My head shook. "I don't understand."

"None of us do. Why don't you go over what you remember with me. I've watched the tapes. The angle isn't the best, but I didn't see anyone slip you anything. The kitchen was clean. Your food was fine. Walk me through that day from the moment you woke up."

Heat burned my cheeks as embarrassment soaked into my deepest parts. Woke up? I barely slept. Dirty. Yes. That's right. I did this. I brought the sickness on myself.

"Slave?"

"I don't want to talk about it. Leave me."

"If I'm going to figure out what happened—"

"Not figure out," I exploded. "Es me. I did this. I..." Sobs made it impossible for me to go on. A door swung open, and my Master stormed out, wet, his towel still around his waist.

"What the fuck is going on here? What did you do?"

The question was aimed at Elec, but my cries only grew. I didn't belong here. I was weak. Sick. I had to pray. I needed to clean myself inside and out. And the apartment. I'd have to clean that too or else this would continue. I'd keep getting sick.

"I only asked her to walk me through her day. She got upset. She said she did this."

"No way, I never left her side. Clara? Shh. No more crying.

We'll figure it out. Tell us what happened. What made you sick?"

All I could do was look at him aghast. My head shook as if he were supposed to know.

"Clara. Slave, please."

"*Don't.* I am not a slave. *You* did this. You and me. I told you this would happen. I told you it's dirty. All of it. Look what we did. I w-want to go home. I'm sick. I need." My words were barely making sense as I cried harder. I was so tired and queasy still. All I wanted to do was go back to sleep and disappear from here forever.

Footsteps left from my side. Moments went by before the bathroom door closed, only to reopen. My Master and Elcc went right into talking.

"She doesn't know. She thinks her superstitions brought this on herself. Rob, I'll watch the tapes again, but I couldn't find anything that might have poisoned her. It wasn't the food from the restaurant. We have every angle of that kitchen recorded. Nothing was done to any of your meals. Are you sure there's nothing you're forgetting?

"I've tried to think. I...I don't know. I can't think of anything."

"Can I watch the video from your apartment?"

"I beg your fucking pardon?"

"Don't look at me like that. Every inch of this place is recorded. It has to be for situations just like this. I haven't looked out of respect for your privacy, but I need to watch. She said she did this. Just in case she's not referring to her religion or views, I need to see for myself."

A sound left my Master. I turned towards them, watching as his stare narrowed at me.

"Do it. Let me know immediately if you come across something."

"I'll call the moment I finish."

Elec gave me one last glance before he left the room. Concern and anger tightened my Master's expression, but he continued towards me, taking a seat on the edge of my bed.

"I'm having Elec watch the video of our apartment. Is there anything you want to tell me before he does?"

"There's nothing to tell. He'll see why this happened when he watches."

"Because what we do is dirty, or because you did this to yourself?"

My eyes studied his as sleep tried to pull me under. My mouth felt heavy and talking seemed so hard to do. "Dirty," I said, waving my hand, but pointing upwards. "Fate. He disapproves. It's my fault. I knew better."

"So, you didn't poison yourself?"

"Poison, no. Karma, yes."

MASTER B-1212

One day. Three days. Five.
Every hour was fucking torture as I watched my slave get further and further away with having anything to do with me. Concern over her wellbeing had kept me from putting my hands on her, but now that she was becoming obsessive in her cleanliness and rituals it was getting to the point where I was quickly running out of patience. And hadn't that used to be my biggest problem? I didn't think; I reacted. I didn't think; I spoke. I didn't think; I did. And we all knew anything I did was never good enough. Not for the public, and not for my impossible, abusive, career-politician father. He hadn't been the best role model, despite what he showed for outward appearances.

To the world, Roger Delgado was without fault. They saw the grief-stricken husband and doting father. They saw a man who spent nearly a year at his wife's bed as she withered away from sickness and cancer, and the son he raised for years on his own after her death. To them, he could do no wrong. What they didn't see was the evidence of his darker side burned all over me. Cigar burn, here. *You're a failure, Robert.* A burn, there. *Did I tell you to use your fucking head? What were you thinking?* A collection of his wrath, all over my chest, thighs, and back. *"You know better than that. Do you see what an embarrassment you are? Did you see the headlines you made? How could you do something so stupid?*

I thought I'd become more patient. After all, I'd taken all the classes. I went through therapy and training to better manage my emotions and reactions for situations. Patience. Empathy. Breathing through the impulses. Analyzing what caused the reaction. Was it rational? Was it the right decision?

I was losing my fucking slave to a stupid belief. One I didn't understand. One I couldn't fathom. Yes, that was worth knocking her straight. Maybe even physically. She had to see she didn't do this to herself, and that's what pissed me off the most. Somehow, somewhere, someone hurt my slave. Maybe not even intentionally, but there was a chance, and I would not rest until I figured out what happened.

"Come on, Clara, time to eat."

"I'm not hungry."

"You barely touched your lunch. You're eating."

"Later. Sick."

"Still? It's been days."

Her eyes closed, and she curled more into herself. I wasn't sure whether to believe her or not. How far did this superstition go? She thought her actions made her sick. Could she be holding to that even though she was fine now...or was she truly not feeling well?

"Up. Come on."

I scooped her into my arms, shoving the bathroom door open. Clara thrashed in my hold, but I refused to put her down.

"What are you doing? Take me back."

"Why, because I'm dirty? Because you think I make you suffer with this sickness?"

"Not Rob. Es me."

Tears filled her eyes as I gave a hard jerk at her word. "Lies. It's not true. And what did I tell you about saying my name. You should have never heard the Main Master call me that. I should beat you for saying it so much." But she did say it, and it made me warm even more towards her. So much so, I wasn't sure what to think about it.

"I want to go back to bed. You have to stay away. I'm sick and you'll get sick like me if you keep touching. You shouldn't even be around me."

"What do we have to do to make you better?"

I finally placed her down, turning on the faucet to fill the tub.

"Nothing. It just is. I've cleaned what I can."

"Then we do it my way. I'll make it disappear. Do you want me to do that?"

"Impossible. How?

Spinning, I went back to the kitchen, grabbing a knife and a lighter. When I returned into the bathroom, Clara's eyes locked right on what I held.

"You'll kill me now? I suppose—"

"Don't be ridiculous. You're going to bleed it out."

She didn't speak as she stared down at what I held.

"I'll bleed. You'll bleed. We'll release whatever is bad and we'll start new. New right now. No past. No nothing. Brand new."

"What is this you say? It's not true. It's make up."

"Make-believe is the word, and no, it's not." I took in the conflict in her tone. It had her words thickening in English, which told me she was truly weighing if it would work. Thing was, I wasn't going to let her get out of this. I pulled my shirt over my head making Clara immediately close her eyes. Her shoulders were caved and despite her lids blocking her view, the tears still made their way free. "See this. It's truth. These right here." I gripped her chin, adding increasing pressure as I waited for her eyes to open. "These circles, they're burns. They tried to cleanse me, and they worked, but they weren't permanent. This though, the knife, it'll erase everything Clara. I helped you before, remember? I made the pain go away."

"But I got sick. I wanted it."

For seconds I couldn't speak.

"Because of the oil?"

"Oil made it worse, but it didn't take my mind, Master. I still wanted it. Now I'm paying for that."

She wanted me too. No force. No persuasion. Just me. "End it. Cut the tie to your past. Bleed it out right now, and start new with me."

Clara studied me skeptically. She wasn't sure whether to believe me, and I didn't blame her. I was so full of shit, desperate to nip this bullshit in the bud once and for all, especially if I could have her again. Have her my way. *Our way.* God, I was sick. Beyond fucked up.

"You're not afraid of pain. I'll cut me first. No more past. Then, I'll cut you. We'll bleed together, and then bathe and get really clean to start over new. What do you think?"

"I think it's lies but—"

My lips crushed into hers. "Not lies. Us. You and me. Master and slave. A new start. We can do this once a month to make sure it keeps working. This can be our way. Say yes."

"If we do this, we do it my way. Both of us in the bath. We'll cut each other and then wash. Not separate, together."

"Deal."

My cock was hard just thinking about splitting open her skin. If we did this monthly, even better. Whatever it would take to get her on normal terms. *My terms.* And then we could continue where we left off. Just…better.

I reached over, turning off the water to the nearly full tub. As

MASTER B-1212

I sterilized the blade, I soaked in Clara getting undressed. She was still slightly pale, but only because I knew she hadn't been sleeping well. I planned to change that tonight. I'd put her to bed good. She'd sleep better than she ever had in her entire life. Come tomorrow, I would hold to my word, and we'd start new. But in a place that fit both of us. Clara could bake or cook. I'd make her cater to me. She'd like that. And me, I'd bask in every fucking minute of seeing her happy. She served. Whether she was a fighter or not, it's what she knew. It's what she described. Breads. Pies. I wanted to see what she was capable of. Of what made her, her.

"There. Where do you want me? In the bath or here?"

"Bath." She reached for the knife and for the longest moment I hesitated. God, she could fucking murder me if she wanted to. Question was...would she try?

"You be careful with that." Reluctantly, I handed it over, not taking my attention from it for a second. I was ready just in case, but I also wanted her to see I was trusting her. It worked as I undressed and climbed in. Clara joined me, sending water nearly sloshing over the side. She stayed on her knees in the deep tub, pointing with the tip to my arm. "Just a small cut. It doesn't have to be deep."

My arm extended as she went between my tanned skin and my face. She seemed just as surprised as I'd been that I'd given her the damn knife to begin with.

"No past. New start."

She bit on her bottom lip as she leveled the tip against my flesh. When she pushed in and blood pooled over metal, she smiled, her gaze jerking up to me.

"Do it a little more. Drag it towards you, slave."

My cock throbbed at the sight. I didn't care for the pain, but bleeding for her, it did something to me. I was so used to having my fantasy play out the other way around. Maybe my past was

69

escaping me. Maybe it was turning into reality. Did I feel lighter? Weightless in our moment?

"Life. Put it in water. Purify."

I obeyed, watching the red swirl free in the clear liquid. It was hypnotizing, just like she was.

"My turn. No more sickness. No more past. Hold out your arm, slave."

She handed me the knife, and I held under her forearm as I leveled the blade in the area she'd placed mine. Clara sucked in at the puncture, watching as I cut along her skin. I nearly dropped the knife and took her right there.

"Wait." I let the tip drag against her, not cutting, but trailing the length towards her wrist. "Since you're the one sick, we're going to make sure. We won't risk this not working." I stopped, pushing through the layers of skin before she could argue. Crimson beaded the small surface, and I angled it to the side to push the tip in once more. A deep inhale sounded but I barely heard. Three wounds. Third time would be the charm.

Blood ran a river over her pale skin, dripping to the water between us. It took seconds to bring my gaze up from the heaven I was existing in.

Drip.

Drip.

Drip.

"Perfect. You're so fucking perfect, slave. Purify. Be mine for real."

"Yours."

It wasn't a question. She was taking the title, freely. Saying it to make it true.

I waited while she put her arm in the water. Mine stung with the contact, but I could have cared less. I reached over, putting the blade on the counter and pulling her into me like I'd wanted now for days. Clara met my lips just as hungrily, driving me past any need I had felt with anyone else.

"Wait. Master. Get your head wet. Go underwater."

Not even letting her go, I turned to my back, sliding down to submerge us both. It was seconds of sating her wish. I was finished with this ritual and with all the bullshit we'd left behind. We were new. Both of us. Somehow, I held to that.

"Bed. *Now.*"

W0023

"Twenty-three, what happened? Are you okay? Master said you were in the hospital again. Did you relapse? Did the sickness come back?"

As I watched slave fifty reach for my hands, I thought about correcting her with my name again, but I'd done that three different times at our last lunch, and twice the one before. I knew better than to fight her training. She wouldn't call me Clara no matter how much I begged her to, which was fine. If I learned anything in the last three weeks, it was that there were some things you couldn't change. This was one of them.

"I'm fine." I slipped my hands back before she could touch them with her energy. "Master just wanted me to go in for a checkup to make sure I was okay."

"And everything's good?"

"Yes. I'm fine."

I took in the dark circles under her eyes, shaking my head as she reached into her purse and offered me a candy from the bag that was hidden inside. I was clean now. I didn't view fifty as dirty in the technical sense, but she was unclean concerning her health. She appeared exhausted. Weak. She even looked as though she'd lost some weight which was alarming. She was already so skinny. Taking the candy she offered was taking her illness, which I was not going to do.

"How are you feeling? Are you sick too?"

She shrugged. "I'm better than I was last week. I think I'm finally bouncing back. Master said an illness was going around so I guess I've just been battling it too. Flu? I don't know. My immune system has never been good. You can guarantee if there's something making people sick, I'll be the first to catch it and the last to have it. Master says I'm lucky to have him with how sickly I am. I think he's right."

"It was no flu for me. There's sickness? Here?" My lids narrowed even more as I watched her chew and swallow. Nervousness hit hard, and my gaze dropped down again to the new candy she brought to her mouth. They were round and chewy, tasting of different fruits. I still had the ones she gave me in my purse from our first visit. I hadn't really been a fan of their taste, so I didn't eat many.

"Oh yes. It's pretty bad from what I hear. Some sort of stomach bug. Something is spreading around. Say, I hear they're putting out the new movies tomorrow, do you want to go see one with me? Do you think your Master would want to go? I've been begging mine and he says if yours agrees, we can all go together."

Her enthusiasm faded for a moment as she stopped mid-chew. Anxiously, I looked over at our Masters. They seemed to be in deep conversation, but mine kept peeking over at me. Maybe he could tell I was uneasy. I didn't like being out around so many people anymore. I was paranoid at anyone who got too close. No matter how hard I tried, I couldn't erase what I'd been taught. There were too many bad energies, and I didn't want to get sick again, even if my poisoning hadn't really come from that.

"I have lots of meal, meals, to make tomorrow, but I'll ask

him." Words shuffled on my tongue, tripping me up as I watched her force herself to swallow. "It sounds fun, though. A movie could be good. Is that where you got your candy?"

Fifty's smile broadened. "Oh, no. You can't buy these at a store. My Master makes them for me."

"No," I said, acting surprised. "He does?"

"Yes. They're my special treat. I get them once a week, and only for the day. I ate way too many the last time and got the worst tummy ache. I even had to get an IV and medicine, I was so sick. Master took such good care of me. He always does. He wasn't too happy that I gave my first bag to you. I didn't even get to try them. I was just so excited we were friends, and I was taught to give gifts when meeting someone new. Do you still have them? I can try to get you more if you already ate them all. I think I have an extra bag in the cupboard. Master cuts me off after I eat a few. He says it'll spoil my dinner, but sometimes I sneak more," she whispered, smiling. "I think he knows, but he never punishes me."

"I…" I leaned in, chewing my lip. I couldn't stop myself from shaking as I kept taking in the candies. For the first time since the injured girl at auction night, I felt it. Fear. True fear. "I still have mine. Do you get sick a lot?"

"Not too much. I mean. I…sometimes. It's this place. It's so full of germs from all the different people coming through. That's what my Master says. I'm so susceptible. I have a weak body. He got me a prescription for some really good multivitamins, so those should help soon."

I couldn't speak as I just stared at her. Surely, she was right. I was just overthinking this. She was fine. I was fine. But I hadn't been after I'd eaten that candy…I'd almost died.

Stealing a look back at the Masters' table, I twisted my long dress in my lap. Should I say something? Leave it alone? Rob would be angry at me if I were wrong. How many times had I reacted for nothing? I was trying to be a good slave, but I kept finding it harder and harder to be out in public not knowing how I'd gotten sick. Did I know now...or was it something else?

"Twenty-three, are you okay?"

I tried to smile, but my lips barely moved as I pointed to her purse. "I overheard the doctor at the hospital say sweets can make the sickness worse. It could be bad if you think about it. Have you tried not eating them? Those ones? Maybe...see what happens?"

Fifty looked down at where I pointed. "Why would my candies make me worse? Master is a doctor. They're special. He said...He...Surely, he'd know if they..." She stopped, staring at the brightly colored candy she held to. She looked back at me, and then back to the candy. Time stretched as she began putting it together.

"Maybe just see? A break could be good."

"I..." She put the one she held back in the bag resting inside her purse. "I can maybe see if it helps." She got quiet too, joining in my silence as we began to stare at each other. There had to be a million things going through both of our minds, but all I knew was I wanted my Master. I wanted to leave.

"Friend, can you come to my place? Maybe help me rest?"

Her head shook, her gaze lowering to the table. "I should go. I'm suddenly not feeling so well either." She stopped, refusing to look back up to me. Despite the inner voice that yelled for me not to touch her, I stood, pulling her hand up to kiss. But only the one not holding to the candy. "Be well. Rest. No sweets for a while, please. Just...be safe. Movies tomorrow, yes?"

She nodded but didn't speak. Maybe I was wrong, but what if I wasn't? What if my Master found out what I'd put in her head and got mad? He would punish me. I just needed time. I had to see what happened to her being off the candy.

"Clara?" I looked over at my name. Rob's hand lifted to the older doctor, and he stood. "Are you okay?"

I headed towards him, nodding as I approached. "I'm tired. I want to go home."

"You are a bit pale." Worry. I saw it the moment my words left me. Rob's arm came out around me, pulling me close. "Sorry to end this so soon; she hasn't been the same the last few weeks. You can tell me more about my dad tomorrow. Same time?"

"Actually," he glanced to fifty, studying her. "I think we had movie plans. Did you both discuss that?"

I forced a smile, not able to stop my nearly convulsive trembling. "Yes. If my Master agrees, it sounds fun. But she's sick. I think your slave needs rest like me."

"Your slave is sick too?"

Rob's head whipped over to fifty.

The doctor laughed. "Nothing serious or to worry about. I hear there's a stomach flu going around. A few people fell ill at dinner last night too. I've been keeping an eye on her. She'll be fine."

"Stomach flu? Great. As if we needed that on top of everything."

"I doubt it lasts long. Lots of handwashing. The store has disinfectant wipes. Those should help too."

"Indeed. I'll be sure to pick some up." My Master looked down as I gripped to him tighter. "We should go. We'll talk tomorrow."

The doctor nodded, and I couldn't get out of there fast enough. I couldn't stop all the questions as they assaulted me. Could fifty's Master really be intentionally getting her sick? And if so, what if she'd have eaten from that first bag. I'd only eaten four and they almost killed me. Had he meant to kill her? Had he lowered the dose of poison for fear of getting caught after I accidently got sick? She was popping her new ones by the handful. I felt nauseous at the thought. My hand shot to my mouth as I tried not to gag.

"Whoa, slave. Fuck. Not again."

My head shook as tears blurred my vision. "Not sick. Not like that. Take me home."

"If you're not sick, what's wrong?"

"*Take me home.*"

And he did. I barely made it inside before I pulled the dress over my head and raced for the shower. Could I accuse a Master of poisoning his slave? Did it matter if he did? We'd been told over the months we were here that we'd probably die. I had been one of the lucky ones, but what about fifty? What if she wasn't? What if her Master was slowly killing her?

The reality of the situation only had me gagging again as I turned on the water. There was literally nothing I could do. I couldn't even help her without condemning myself.

"*Slave.*"

The threat in his tone sent tears racing down my cheeks. I was going to be in so much trouble. What if fifty told her Master what I insinuated? What if he hurt her for it?

"Talk to me. What is wrong with you?"

My head shook, and the sob was automatic.

"You don't want to tell me?"

Again my hair went bouncing around my face at the shake.

"But there's something you're hiding?"

Both my hands pressed over my mouth as I spun in a circle. No one was safe here. Not really. Not even me. My Master was going to leave eventually, and then what would happen? No, I wouldn't fall into that trap of helplessness. I was a Bordelli. I was strong.

I took a shuddering breath, trying to calm the waves of panic.

"Are you ready to tell me?"

"Es nothing."

"You're lying; you can't even talk straight. Slave, you know how this works. No shower until you release what you're hiding. Pick your method. Either way, you're coming clean. I won't have

77

you sick again, and we know what will happen if you keep this from me. Do you want to invite evil to us?"

There it was, more sobs. My head shook.

"Release and purify. Which one?"

"Bad."

"It's bad? How bad?"

My finger shook as I pointed to the lighter that rested on the counter. One of Rob's eyebrows lifted in surprise but quickly turned to concern. He headed over, pulling me in his arms.

"What the hell did the two of you talk about? I saw you both shut down. Spill it, Clara."

As he led me to the counter, I eyed the shower. I wanted to clean myself so bad I couldn't stand it. That couldn't happen until I either bled out, burned it out, or Master released it through my pain.

"She's sick."

"I know. I heard."

Quicker my head shook, and I held out my arm letting it bounce with my impatience. Rob's lips tightened but he pushed down the lighter, angling it so the sides heated up.

"She's sick. Why is that so bad? You heard him, it's a flu. People are getting sick all over. Do you think it's their bad deeds that are bringing on the sickness? Is that what this is about?"

"No. I think. *Hurry.*"

"Not until you get it out."

A sound left me as I raced to the closet to grab my purse. When I came back with the candy, my Master let the flame die. He stared at it, looking between me and the bag.

"You were eating those."

"Yes."

"At the restaurant…before you got sick."

"Yes."

Rob's head cocked the slightest amount. "I didn't buy those for you. Where did you get them?"

"Friend. He made them for her. It's a special candy. He made them; he didn't buy. And she's sick too. He got mad at her when she gave them to me. I think…" I wiped the flowing tears away. "He made her more. She was eating them in front of me just now and she went from happy to…sick. I think—"

My Master snatched the bag, grabbing the phone from his pocket. He laid both on the counter, staring at them. Moments went by before he picked back up the lighter, letting it burn.

"Arm."

I lifted it, biting down as the blistering pain seared into my skin. I cried out, my other fist flying to my mouth as the hot metal sizzled through my flesh.

"I release you of your secret. Never speak of it again. Not to her. Not to anyone."

MASTER B-1212

"Rob, you know I want to help, but truthfully there's nothing I can do. Had I saw the girl slip your slave the bag of candy under the table, we probably would have solved this faster, but they're slaves, and it was an accident. Other than fining Master Sixty-three for allowing his slave to carry something that lethal outside of his apartment, my hands are tied. It's just the way things are here."

I paced in front of the Main Master, understanding what he said but not liking any of it.

"But it was the candy? You tested it for poison?"

"I did, it was positive. Had he intentionally given them to your slave this would be a completely different story. He'd die, plain and simple, but slave fifty did this and not even intentionally." Elec shrugged. "You're just going to have to be careful when you're both out. These Masters down here are into things you've probably never even heard of. This just happens to be what Sixty-three is into. I knew this before he ever stepped foot on the grounds. It's part of our application process. Complete honesty. He nurses slaves to death. He's a caregiver to the very end. It is what it is."

"Weeks ago when my slave got poisoned, he offered me medication under the table. Anything I wanted or needed. Not a big deal, but then he mentioned that there's a flu going around. He laughed. It was so out of place. I've been asking around. What about the outbreaks in the different restaurants? Do you not find these sicknesses appearing around food suspicious at all? Is it just me? I'm afraid to even order out anymore. I don't trust him, Elec. The man...he's never felt right. I've tried letting it go because our slaves are friends, but fuck. I just can't shake the way he makes me feel."

The Main Master's finger thrummed against the desk as his lids narrowed the smallest amount. To read him was impossible. He looked from me to the wall of glass that gave view to the city below. His floor and the guard apartments across the city were the only one giving a glimpse to the chaos that made up this place.

"You think he's intentionally making people sick?"

"I'm progressing, being here at the Gardens. I've done things to my slave I'd never have the balls to try outside of this place. Why couldn't he? What's one slave or many masters when faced with someone who just wants to see people sick?" My hand pushed back my hair from my forehead. "I know you have a lot of shit you're overlooking at this place, but I have a bad feeling about George. I don't want to accuse him of anything, but I think this should be investigated. If he is poisoning people, he's not going to stop. Right now, the symptoms are manageable, but what happens when he wants them to be worse?"

Elec stood from the desk, walking to the wall of glass. He placed his hands behind his back as he stared down.

"I won't say him doing something like that never crossed my mind. My job is to think of every scenario possible. I weigh the risk, and I go from there. His risk was higher than I liked, but I had to see where he stood. Everyone is different; their compul-

A. A. DARK

sions rarely are. Whether they elevate, and how high is something I can't calculate. Not in a place like this."

"Will you at least look into it?"

The Main Master turned to me, anger shadowing his face. "I had lunch on the main floor with my High Leader and a few of the guards last week in the food court. It wasn't planned, but let's say we felt the effects of this flu. Bet your ass I'm going to investigate it."

A sigh of relief left me. "Thank you. I hope I'm wrong. In case I'm not, I'm glad you're going to check into it. I should go. I can't stand leaving Clara alone. Thanks, Main Master."

Closing the door behind me, I kept my steps at a fast pace. The elevator ride down from the top floor took forever. It was as if everyone decided to leave at the exact same moment. I only had four floors to travel, but we stopped at every damn one as people piled in or got off. When I finally stepped onto the sixteenth floor, all I felt was relief. I hadn't been gone maybe a half hour, give or take. It didn't matter. Five minutes away from my slave with Master Sixty-three loose was too damn much. From the moment she showed me that candy...I knew. I didn't want to believe it, but I'd always been cautious around him, from the first time I'd really met him as my mother's doctor. No one was so nice without harboring a bad secret, and his was worse than I had imagined. It made my skin crawl. It ground my insides with questions I wasn't sure I should think about. Killing his slave slowly. Slow...like my mother. That took such a low level of emotion I hadn't gotten to yet. Hurting my slave, yes, I could do that. Killing her, and not just taking her life, but dragging it out for a long period of time, no way. I saw my mother suffer for almost a year. That wasn't something I was capable of.

I grabbed the card from my pocket, sliding it in and opening the door. Before the barrier shut, intuition told me something was wrong. It wasn't the silence or even the absence of my slave, it was the energy. Something I'd heard Clara speak about since I'd gotten her. It was wrong. The hair was standing up on my arms, and my pulse was picking up, slamming into me with every step I took.

"Slave?"

Pushing the card into my pocket, I headed for the bedroom. My ears perked, taking in everything from the patting of my shoes on wood, to carpet once I entered. The bed was empty. I threw the closet open, rushing to the bathroom. Nothing.

"Clara. *Slave.*" I spun, running for the door. The minute I opened it, I jerked to a stop. "Father."

"You don't look very happy to see me. What's the matter, making yourself at home?"

"You could say that. Come in." I waved him inside, more switching out position so I didn't have him in the way of the door. "You're going to have to wait here. I have to find my slave."

"No need." He took the fedora from his head, revealing white hair. His piercing brown eyes never left me as he held to the hat, keeping it in his grip as he dropped his hands.

"You know where Clara's at?"

"I do."

"*Well?* Where is she?"

"With George, of course. He said you all had plans to go to the movies. She didn't want to go, but I assured her you wouldn't care. After all, we needed to talk anyway."

"You didn't..." My head shook and I didn't stand around to hear another word. I pulled my phone from my pocket, running for the elevator at full speed. I had no idea where the movie theater was. As I scanned the large map bolted to a pillar not feet away, the phone rang.

"Come on. *Come on!*"

"*Leave a message.*"

"Elec, call me back, *now.*"

"Where the fuck is it?" My eyes were jerking all over the

map. There were so many floors. "Theater." I spun in a circle, taking in the random Master heading into the small shops filling our lobby area. "Theater! Anyone know the floor?" Eyes flickered to me, but no one spoke.

A sound left me as I hit redial, cursing. A Master and slave headed towards one of the halls, and my hand shot out. "Theater. Do you know what floor it's on?"

The slave's mouth opened but she didn't speak as she glanced at her Master who shrugged.

"You know. Slave, what floor? This is an emergency. *Please.*"

The young girl immediately looked to her Master for approval. At the nod, I let out a deep breath. One I didn't even know I had been holding.

"Fourth floor, Sir, towards the left."

"Thank you!"

The elevator was opening, and I barely made it through the doors as it began closing. Repeatedly, I pressed the button. At my phone ringing, I jumped, fumbling with it as it bounced around my hands.

"Elec? Hello, Elec?"

"Rob, calm down, what's going on?"

"My father." I could barely catch my breath. "He sent Clara with Sixty-three. If he knows that she knows…that I know, or you—"

"Got it. Where are they?"

"The theater. I'm on the elevator now."

"I'll have the guards try to intercept in case you don't make it there fast enough." He paused as I waited for him to come back on. "Alright, they're going to find her now. I'll start checking the cameras. Don't let Sixty-three see you upset. We don't want to tip him off that we're suspicious."

I broke from the door the moment it opened. "Got it. I'm on

the fourth floor now. I'm going to try to find this place. I'll call you back when I have her."

Hanging up, I started to head left like the slave said, quickly finding out it wasn't that simple. The floor was opened, and there were lines formed going into different showings. I had no idea what movie they'd chosen to see.

"Clara?" I called out her name, pushing through people as I searched out red hair. With as short as she was, it was impossible to see over the masses that were waiting to get in. "Clara! Slave!"

Heads turned, but I didn't pay them any attention. I made it to the front, pushing the remaining way to the concession stand.

"Hey. Hey you. Slaves!" At the roar of my voice, the three wearing yellow headdresses turned to view me. "I need you to page my slave. Her name is Clara. Tell her to come to the front to meet her Master."

A short, dark-haired girl nodded, coming feet towards me as she picked up a phone.

"Slave Clara, please come to the concession stand, your Master is waiting for you. Slave Clara, please come to the concession stand."

"*Thank you.*" I stepped back, spinning and taking in all the entrances, praying she'd hurry and come out. Guards pushed their way in, here and there. I knew they were looking for her as well. Minutes passed. Longer. Panic had me sweating as I jerked the phone back to my ear. It was answered immediately.

"Elec, I had her called over the speaker. She's not coming. I can't find her."

"Stay there. *Do not leave.* I'm looking into some leads now. I'll call you when I know something."

W0023

"Don't be shy. I know this isn't your house, but you're family here. I mean, after all, your Rob's slave. I've known Rob since his elementary days. I've practically watched him grow. Did you know I was his father's doctor for over ten years before he became vice-president? I even attended to Janey when she got sick. That was fun. We were all so close. We would have been closer had I accepted his father's proposal to join him at the Naval Observatory, but how could I do that and be here at the same time, you know?"

A sob left me as I stole a peek over to fifty. She was slumped to the side in her chair, foam seeping from her mouth and trailing down her chin. The white of her eyes were dotted red with broken blood vessels, and I couldn't stop jumping and crying out every time she twitched and jerked.

"Please. I want to go home. My Master—"

"He's busy, child. Did you not hear his father? The two men have his future to discuss. They don't need you in the way while they talk. Eat. Be a good girl. I'd hate to have to sedate you even more."

"I...can't. I'm not hungry...I want to go home."

"If you run for that door again, you'll get more than punishment and a shot. That hit to your cheek was only a warning. In this house, we obey or there's consequences. I won't choke you like your Master, but I can steal some of your air so you can't breathe. Do I need to do that? I have a shot for that."

It took everything I had to shake my head. I was so heavy, and I couldn't stop the sobs. Why hadn't I run before this? Why didn't I make them drag me from the apartment kicking and screaming? I hadn't wanted to come at all, but Rob's father practically pushed me out. How he even got a key to begin with was beyond me. I'd been so excited when the door opened, thinking it was my Master, but when I saw the older man, panic set in. He was a stranger, and he was in our home. He didn't seem the least bit phased by my fear. He stood with the door opened, talking to Sixty-three as if they'd known eachother forever, which it appeared they did,

"Please." I sniffled, squaring my shoulders as best as I could. "I would like permission to call my Master. He needs to know I'm here and safe. He will not be happy when he finds out I left. Please, it's an emergency for me. I'm expected..." I sobbed so hard I could barely continue. "I'm a good slave. Let me make my Master happy."

"You're a good slave?" His arms crossed over his chest as he stared me down. "You weren't the first night I saw you; you were running."

"I learned. I'm better now. I'm good."

"Perhaps you've changed your stripes. Then again, you're still not eating, so I highly doubt it."

"But...you're not my Master. Master has a schedule like you. I already ate. I can't have more."

His eyes narrowed as he continued to try to read me. I felt sick as my stomach rolled. I had no idea what he'd shot me up with but with every minute that went by, I felt even more tired and nauseous. After what I saw fifty go through, I prayed my

A. A. DARK

fate wasn't the same. I couldn't die like this. I wasn't ready to leave my Master. We'd bled for each other. We'd purged out the past...for what? For a worse future? Was this the price I was now having to pay?

"Master, please. Can I call to tell him I'm okay?"

Harder his stare became as he glared.

"Maybe I can't blame you since you're basically an illegal, but you must have some common sense. Rob's father is the Vice-President of the United States. *Vice-President.* Second most important man in our country. You really want me to allow you, a slave, to call and interrupt their meeting?"

"My Master will be angry if I don't. Please. I'll make it quick. I beg you."

"Eat."

"*I will not!*"

I forced myself to my feet, falling two steps in my race for the front door. My adrenaline only got me so far, and it wasn't far at all. The room was beginning to spin, and bile was burning the back of my throat as I clawed to the wooden floor.

"I knew it wouldn't be much longer. Let's get to the part where we talk about the candy my slave gave you."

Pressing my toes into the floor, I felt myself inch the smallest amount. My arms were barely working anymore. The chair slid against the wood, and the reverberation of footsteps vibrated through my entire being.

"My slave told me what you said. Does he know? Did you tell your Master that's how you got sick?"

"No." I forced the answer, pulling at the floor as I moved the smallest amount.

"Are you sure? I know Rob went to talk to Elec. Is he there because of me? What does he know?"

"Nothing," I sobbed. "I know...nothing what...you say. P-Please."

"I'm afraid I don't believe you. I think you know exactly

88

what I'm talking about. I also think Rob went to inform the Main Master, and that wouldn't be a very good thing at all if they started poking around. Do you know how long I've waited to get into a place like this? What I've done to get here?"

Another inch. Two. He stood between me and the door, but I couldn't stop moving. If I did, I was afraid I wouldn't be able to continue moving at all.

"I told...no one. Just let me go."

The last was but a jumbled breath as another pinch registered into the side of my throat. My nails sunk into the room, and I tried to scream, to beg, but all I heard was laughter. *Crazed laughter.* I was so weak. Heavy. My head wouldn't even lift as I stared across the sideways living room into what had to be the bedroom. It was dark, but everything was starting to fade the smallest amount. My sight. My breath. All I wanted was Rob. To go back to my new home. A home I'd only just accepted with rules I swear I could live by if I only had a little more time. I'd be good. I'd do anything.

"You're lying. He knows. They all know." He crouched, a long sigh leaving him as he began to stroke my hair. "It's okay. Let go and sleep. Shut your eyes, child. I'll take care of you. Trust me; I'm a doctor."

MASTER B-1212

mbrace. Hadn't that been the reason I'd been brought here to the Gardens? Hadn't that been what Elec had told me to do? To embrace this monstrosity inside me? Embrace. It's the only thing that kept going through my head as I raced down my hall, right towards Master Sixty-three's room. Guards were already piled outside of the door, and from the look on Elec's face as he saw me heading right for them, I knew it wasn't good. He was talking to another man. One in a suit. I'd seen the person before, and I was pretty sure I was looking at the Main Board Member. Just seeing them together with their grim faces killed me.

My world flipped. My heart split in two. My feet never slowed.

"Master Twelve-twelve."

Calm. Dead calm. He was in business mode. Elec's arm came out to stop me as I headed for the door, but I slapped it away, trying to push through the guards that were blocking the barrier like a barricade.

"Clara! Slave!"

"Rob."

90

"*No.* Clara! Don't make me fight my way in there. Slave, you get out here right now. Clara!"

"Rob."

"No! Make them move. I want my slave. She's in there, isn't she?"

It was only then that I finally tore my sight off the entrance. No matter how hard I grabbed or tried pushing through the guard, they wouldn't budge. The only way I was making it through was if the man before me, my friend—my Main Master, gave them permission.

"My slave, Elec. Where's Clara?"

Blue eyes. They were as deep as the ocean as he stared at me. What was in their depths, I didn't have a clue. A monster? A void? Maybe I'd never know. I wasn't sure if Elec could feel my pain, or if he was beyond feeling anything at all. We'd been close in college, but what happened to him the last decade, there was no telling. With what he did now, I was guessing whatever it was wasn't good.

"Clara is all but dead. I'm sorry. If I make them move, you have two choices. One, you prove me wrong and show me you can detach. That you can be rational. You can let me hold a public execution to make an example out of Master Sixty-three. You'll move to alpha status as Master and come and go as you please. Or two, you admit to me and Master Lemmons you're beyond control, and we'll let you kill him in this room here and now…but you never leave. Not ever. The choice is yours."

"My slave is dead?"

"We have people working on her now, but I'm afraid whatever the doctor's given her has done its job."

"Let me in."

"Rob, think about this. You can never leave if you kill him."

"Let. Me in."

The words would barely push through my clenched teeth. Every inch of me was tight. Rigid and ready to shatter and break into jagged pieces. I bounced on my feet, pulling at a guard until he finally stepped to the side at Elec's gesture.

Curls. I only caught a glimpse of them in my peripheral as I met George's stare and launched right for the man who was standing between two guards. Maybe I expected him to cower or apologize. He'd always been over-apologetic in the outside world, but here it wasn't the case. The brown eyes were hard, almost as if nothing were behind them at all.

"She did nothing to you. She did nothing! *She was mine.*" I gripped to his shirt, slamming my fist into his face. His head snapped back at the force, but I was already punching his nose and mouth again. At him starting to fall down, I grabbed to his shirt, jerking and pushing him into the kitchen. His smaller body flew at my push, and I swung his light frame into the ground as I jerked open the drawers, reaching for the first knife I saw. Fists swung, but he was far from a fighter.

"She had no right to tell. I deserved to be here. I *paid* for this place."

"We've all fucking paid. Do you know who paid the most?" I slashed through the button up shirt he wore, slicing through his arm that kept coming up trying to fend me off. "My slave! Do you see her? Do you see what you've done?"

"It's nothing compared to what I've had to do outside of here. You have no idea the deeds one must commit to be seen by the right people. I *deserve* my place as Master."

I drug him closer, catching glimpses of her ghostly face and her opened eyes as the Garden's doctor and nurse kept working on her. Flashes of my mother, dying on a hospital bed in our guest room, hit me hard. Gone. Dead eyes. Porsha, as I fucked her countless different times while she lay there like a ghost, so out of it on drugs. Gone too, in her own way. Hollow eyes. Feeling the two pulled as one, and now seeing my slave the same way, it did something to my anger, twisting it to a raw grief I knew too well. The emotion didn't last. It mixed, warping with a sensation that was different altogether. Lust. I nearly went limp with disbelief. The shock at how dark I was going didn't stick around. It escalated off the charts with rage and denial as I flipped the Master to his back before me.

"Look at her, George. Watch her."

My fist connected with his cheek and my mother came back, staring right at me, just not seeing what was before her. But I saw George, hovering in the background like always. A grin edged on his face at every gaze her way. He'd been talking to my dad, and he wanted to smile. I saw it. There was no hiding his underlining pleasure as he took her in. It made me hit him again. And again. Three times.

A sound forced it way through my tight throat, and I switched hands, slicing into his arm again. I waited for him to draw it close, just like I knew he would. It came to cradle against him, and I let my arm stab down right into his chest. Right into the one part of me that was aching with so much loss. Popping blew through my hand like a shock wave, and I kept trying to push deeper as I sliced through layers of muscle. A yell pierced the air, only feeding me as I pulled the five-inch blade free, stabbing down again. Blood spewed past the doctor's lips, splashing against my forearms as I heave the knife in repeatedly.

"You can't see. You'll never see, but you have to." I grabbed the collar of his shirt, barely catching Elec at the door as I pulled him a foot from my slave's face and flipped him on his stomach. My hand clamped to his jaw as I stretched his neck, staring at my slave. At what I wanted back more than anything.

"You tried taking her from me just like you did my mother, didn't you? All for what? Why!"

Nothing but mumbled, wet words. My knee came to settle in the middle of his back, and I pulled up, extending his neck as far as it would go through my hate. George's arms went wild as he tried to fight my hold and breathe at the same time. "It was so important for you to be here, and yet you let your impulses overpower you. It wasn't her fault you got out of hand, but you punished her for your mistake, George, and now she's going to be the last thing you ever see. You wanted this life. You wanted to be part of the Masters. Now you'll die like one. Welcome to the Gardens'."

Blood sprayed over fair skin, dotting my slave's beautiful face as I sawed through Sixty-three's throat with the serrated edge. Gasps and deep inhaling gurgled as the Master's body flopped in my hold. I didn't allow either of us to move as he fought for the last ounce of his life. He'd see her until he wasn't alive to. *I...saw her. Those eyes. Seeing, pulling me in, wanting me to stay as I continued to try to cut off the doctor's head. She wanted me to take care of her like I did with my mother. Like I did with Porsha when she was out of it. She had me here, now. She had me with her forever.

VOICES. NO MATTER HOW MANY DIFFERENT ONES BUZZED around me, I heard nothing at all. I couldn't as I stared into the unresponsive face of my slave. Elec tried checking on me a few times. Even my father could tell I was too far gone. Nothing made sense and yet, I'd never seen anything clearer.

Beep. Beep.

The steady repetition of the machine should have given me hope. After all, it was still going. There was still a pulse, but that was it. They said she'd never return. That she was gone from me for good. What were the odds of that? Of two women closely resembling each other, in love with me, practically dead... because of me. The odds had to be astronomical. I kept trying to figure it out, but all I could see was how I was the common denominator. Me.

"I don't know what to tell you, Mr. Delgado, Rob made his choice. He knew the—"

"Bullshit. I don't care what he chose. My son is not staying here. It's time he comes home. This is my fault. He's here because of me. I made the wrong decision. He hasn't left that girl in days. He won't go through what I did. This was all a big mistake."

"Perhaps it was, but it's too late to worry about that. Rob's already signed the paperwork. Prepare the outside world for his death. He's not leaving here. As Main Master, I refuse to let him. Look at him, he's lost. Fucking gone. He's a liability, and the Gardens won't risk it. This decision is final. Figure out the way you want him to die, and my people will take care of it. You're free to visit him whenever you wish, but he will never leave this place again."

"Do you know who I am? You can't do this."

"I assure you I can. If you'd like to argue, we can start planning a double funeral. Like I mentioned before, the Garden doesn't accept risk. Do you understand me, Vice-President?"

"Don't listen to them, slave. They'll leave again soon." I whispered inches from her face, brushing my lips over her warm cheek. When I nuzzled in, I could have moaned from having her so close. I missed her. I wanted her back, but it's not like I still didn't have her as mine. "A few more days, and we'll get you set up at home. This is going to be fun. A new adventure. Me, you. Think about it."

I sure was. Our life together now was the only thing on my mind. It was my fault we'd gotten here, and I accepted responsibility for that. But I also harbored parts I couldn't admit to myself yet. All I could face was, it was all going to be great. It wouldn't be the same as before, but we'd figure it out. I was committed. I was going to see this through to the end. The important parts wouldn't change. We'd keep our rules—our rituals, and if it ever came time in the far future to get another slave, we'd even teach her how things were meant to be. After all, why fuck up perfection? Never again. This time we'd just be more careful of who we went around. Trust was gone, but even that was more convenient. As long as we stayed away from the others, we'd be safe.

"Now that we're going to be spending our days together, I think we should get to know each other a little bit better. Slave, did I ever tell you the story of my mother? It's a long story. Not short at all. You see, she was beautiful. Strong. She had this elegance and grace to her. An aura very much like you. She was the perfect example of what a woman should be. Everyone thought so, but she got sick. She ended up a lot like you are now, in bed. Sedated, but waiting. My father, he never left her side through her sickness. And when I say never, I mean mostly never. The memories of what I saw…what I heard…they used to give me nightmares, but don't worry, any dirtiness you feel, I'll take care of it for you. *For both of us*. You may like this story despite that it's not conventional. I mean, I didn't understand it either until now."

I kissed her cheek again, moving more towards her mouth as I cupped her face. "The more that I think of it, the more fitting it seems. You spoke of karma. Of fate." Again, I brushed my lips over hers, this time harder, more passionate. "What do you think of history repeating itself? Do you think that's possible? I'm starting to. Perhaps my mother's last days weren't as bad as I had thought. After all, she was the only one my father really loved, and I think I could have loved you had we had more time together. Maybe a part of me already does."

The End

ABOUT THE AUTHOR

Alaska Angelini is a Bestselling Author of dark, twisted happily-ever-afters. She currently resides in Mississippi but moves at the drop of a dime. Check back in a few months and she's guaranteed to live somewhere new.

Obsessive, stalking, mega-alpha hero's/anti-heroes are her thing. Throw in some rope, cuffs, and a whip or two and watch the magic begin.

If you're looking to connect with her to learn more, feel free to email her at alaska_angelini@yahoo.com, or find her on Facebook.

WHEN DARK IS WHAT YOU'RE CRAVING... Step into Pitch Black with Alaska's International Bestselling pen, A. A. Dark.

OTHER TITLES FROM THIS AUTHOR

A.A Dark books

24690 series in Reading Order:

24690 (24690 series, book 1)

White Out (24690 series, book 2)

27001 (Welcome to Whitlock, 24690 series, book 2.1)

27009 (Welcome to Whitlock, 24690 series, book 2.2)

27011 (Welcome to Whitlock, 24690 series, book 2.3)

Or

Welcome to Whitlock Complete Novella Series (book 3)

Black Out (24690 series, book 4)

Garden of the Gods

(all standalones and can be read in any order.)

Mistress B-0003 (Garden of the Gods)

Anna Monroe and Boston Marks in suggested Reading Order

Never Far

Mad Girl (Anna Monroe series, book 1)

MasterMind (An Anna Monroe and Never Far crossover)

Heart Lines (Anna Monroe and Boston Marks)

Crossed Paths- Coming Soon!

Alaska Angelini books

Unbearable

Insufferable

SLADE: Captive to the Dark

BLAKE: Captive to the Dark

GAIGE: Captive to the Dark

LILY: Captive to the Dark, Special Edition 1

CHASE: Captive to the Dark

JASE: Captive to the Dark

The Last Heir

Watch Me: Stalked

Rush

Dom Up: Devlin Black 1

Dom Fever: Devlin Black 2

This Dom: Devlin Black 3

Dark Paranormal/Sci-Fi lover? Check out Alaska's other reads...

Wolf (Wolf River 1)

Prey: Marko Delacroix 1

Blood Bound: Marko Delacroix 2

Lure: Marko Delacroix 3

Rule: Marko Delacroix 4

Reign: Marko Delacroix 5

Sci-Fi

Atlas Lost

Acknowledgments

To my wonderful betas:
Karen Preiato
Nicole Johnson
Devon Brugh
Kayla Cramer
Morgen Frances
Monica Anne Patrie
Elizabeth Jansen
Amy Martin

To my crew! To my rock: Dee Trejo and Nadine Flotte. I love
you all!

GET MORE GARDEN OF THE GODS!

Mistress B-0003 Available now!
Couple B-0001 *Coming Soon!*

NOTES

PROLOGUE

1. A subterranean fortress housing trafficked slaves. You can read about it in the 24690 series by A. A. Dark.
2. Virgin slave. Wears a white robe during the auction. Not capitalized to show slave status.
3. Nonvirgin slave. Wears a blue robe during the auction. Not capitalized to show slave status.
4. Docile, drugged slave. Can be W or B. Heavily trained. Good for elderly or those with disabilities. Not capitalized to show slave status.
5. Ruined, disfigure slaves. Breeders. Convicts fall into this category. Women or men that fall into the breeding category. Black robe during the auction. Usually the cheapest slaves.
6. Mostly male slaves who have undergone forced indoctrination through various scientific methods. (Brainwashing, programming, training, etc.) They're programmed to be focused solely on their Mistress or Master. They are made to be obedient, loyal, and protective.
7. The Main Master from Whitlock, a subterranean fortress housing trafficked slaves. You can read about it in the 24690 series by A. A. Dark.

MASTER B-1212

1. Virgin slave. Wears a white robe during the auction.
2. Docile, drugged slave. Can be W or B. Heavily trained. Good for elderly or those with disabilities.

W0023

1. Docile, drugged slave. Can be W or B. Heavily trained. Good for elderly or those with disabilities.
2. Docile, drugged slave. Can be W or B. Heavily trained. Good for elderly or those with disabilities.

MASTER B-1212

1. Docile, drugged slave. Can be W or B. Heavily trained. Good for elderly or those with disabilities.

Made in the USA
Middletown, DE
01 June 2025

76397582R00064